To B.

GW00793015

The
Ghosteleers

PHILIP BEICKEN

Happy Adventures!

Philip Beicken

~~Hashtag~~ PRESS

Published in Great Britain by Hashtag Press 2019

Text © Philip Beicken 2019
Cover Illustration © Alexandra Artigas 2019
Cover Design © Helen Braid 2019

The moral right of the author has been asserted

All rights reserved. No part of this publication may be reproduced, stored in a retrieval system, or transmitted, in any form or by any means without the prior written permission of the publisher, nor be otherwise circulated in any form of binding or cover other than that in which it is published and without a similar condition being imposed on the subsequent purchaser.

All characters in this publication are fictitious and any resemblance to real persons, living or dead, is purely coincidental.

A CIP catalogue for this book is available from the British Library.

ISBN 978-1-9998053-9-5

Typeset in Garamond Classic by Blaze Typesetting

Printed in Great Britain by Clays Ltd, Elcograf S.p.A.

Hashtag PRESS

Hashtag Press Ltd
Kent, England, United Kingdom
Email: info@hashtagpress.co.uk
Website: www.hashtagpress.co.uk
Twitter: @hashtag_press

To Tracy, Sophia & Finley
(and of course my cat, Morph)
for being my inspiration

Acknowledgements

Thank you to everyone who has supported me in creating this book. Special thanks to Sam Watkins, author of 'Creature Teacher' for great words of wisdom, Daisy White, Author of 'Remember Me' for wonderful encouragement, Bridget and James Cordy for their positive enthusiasm and the very hardworking Helen and Abiola at Hashtag Press.

Special mention to the children and staff at St Mary's C of E Aided Primary School in Pulborough for their very warm welcome.

Finally, I'd like to thank my parents for their unwavering support.

Chapter 1

The Surprise

The explosion literally lifted the roof off the peaceful suburban house. In the garden, Richie the gnome tumbled into the murky pond and Miss Owen's underwear caught fire on the washing line next door. Thick smoke billowed into the grey sky, as Norman's simple furnishings transformed into a charcoaled mess.

Earlier that day, Norman had sniffed the air suspiciously. A distinct smell of gas lingered ominously in the room, but he couldn't figure out where it was coming from. He looked down at his seven-year-old, black Devonshire Rex cat, Morph, as if expecting him to provide the answer.

Morph interrupted licking his black wiry coat and stared at Norman with his large, dark brown eyes. He returned Norman's gaze with a 'give me some chicken or I will start to eat your leg' stare.

Morph had had a busy day trying to get some sleep as

Norman performed his yearly spring clean on his small, badly laid out terrace house.

"I just don't understand where that smell is coming from," Norman muttered, ruffling his brown coloured hair, that always resembled a mop regardless of how it was combed.

He peered around the back of the antiquated freestanding gas cooker. It was still far from gleaming, but at least the eight chips, four peas, one chicken nugget and the single black sock that had somehow escaped from the washing machine, had been cleared away.

He could hear a faint hissing noise, which he didn't remember being there when he had moved the cooker earlier that day. It sounded very much like a deflating balloon that stubbornly refused to give up its last breath.

Morph stuck out his short-haired paw and started to jab Norman's leg like a prize fighter.

Hello? Hungry cat still here! About to starve unless you feed me this instant!

Frustrated at being interrupted, Norman turned his attention to Morph, picked up the empty red chicken bowl and glanced across at his gleaming silver biscuit bowl that had laid untouched for the last three days.

"If you're that hungry, why don't you eat your biscuits?"

A look of distain crossed Morph's round face. *Chicken, now!*

Norman had rescued Morph at six months old and he understood very well the levels of vengeance that Morph could inflict upon him if he didn't get his delicately sliced chicken breast pieces on time. This would consist of being sick on all the fluffy pillows in the house, escaping from the downstairs lounge to sit on Norman's head in the early hours of the morning, or tripping him up at every opportunity (which had once resulted in Norman landing in the goldfish tank and getting Bert stuck up his nose).

Norman caught his reflection in the mirror next to the fridge, or 'chicken world' as it was often called. He raised his arms and flexed his biceps with all of his strength. Nothing. Not even a slight bump creased his worn-out but incredibly comfy navy checked pyjamas. He didn't mind. He liked the fact that he was considered average in height and weight. It was just a shame he was below average in school and hadn't managed to rid himself of the startled gormless look he'd inherited from his father.

To alleviate the gloom in the kitchen, Norman stretched out his index finger to the brushed chrome dimmer switch and pressed it firmly. An instant later, there followed a loud crack and a whoosh that engulfed the whole room.

In a split second, the blast propelled a shocked looking Morph in the direction of Norman and planted his soft underbelly squarely on his face.

The last memory Norman had of his twenty-three years as a human, was his cat glued to his own surprised face, whilst being hurtled across his clean house in a massive, expanding ball of explosive fire.

Chapter 2

The Awakening

Norman blinked slowly and opened his heavy eyes. He found himself lying on top of a spongy, thin, single bed staring at an unfamiliar ceiling, with no features other than a bare light hanging limply.

The bed covers were pale green and felt so crisp that Norman was scared he might break them. Sluggishly, he raised his body on to his elbows and looked around the room.

The cream-coloured walls were unremarkable and plain with no pictures or windows. Situated to his left stood a cheap, wooden, bedside table, where his favourite retro Casio watch had been neatly positioned. Norman noticed the digits were not moving, as if time itself had frozen.

A single occupied chair was positioned in the far corner of the small room, away from the rest of the furniture.

Beaming at Norman, sat a short, ball-shaped man whose

hair seemed to have slipped from the top of his head and appeared to be trying to escape from his nose and ears.

"Ah, welcome, my dear friend. I'm so glad you're able to join us," he said jovially.

He raised himself from the chair with no little degree of effort and stood with a cheerful expression plastered on his chubby, endearing face. In his hand lay a well-worn pamphlet that he kept turning over nervously, as if it intended to bite him at any minute.

"I expect you have one or two questions, but perhaps, maybe, you would permit me to explain a few details?" he suggested. "I think this may help set the scene."

The balding man quickly stepped in Norman's direction and stretched his clammy hand out to place the pamphlet on the bedside table, next to the watch. Then, he hurriedly retreated to the safety of his chair.

Norman sat upright, leaning against the bare wooden headrest and carefully picked up the booklet from the bedside table. In big, bold, dark letters across the front page were the words,

YOU'RE DEAD. GET OVER IT

He stared in disbelief at the words, reading them over and over again, not quite able to comprehend their meaning. He assumed it was a joke and he was really in a private hospital somewhere exotic, about to be surprised by a nurse in a gleaming white uniform.

He opened the booklet to pages two and three, but they

were blank. Nothing appeared but white, empty space. Pages four, five, six... in fact, all the remaining pages, were completely bare.

Norman snapped his head up and looked questioningly at the anxious man facing him, who simply shrugged apologetically and held out his hands.

"It used to be filled with lots of useful information, but we found that after new residents read the front page, they didn't really take any notice of the rest, so I had the words removed. It saves ink, which is one of my better cost-cutting ideas," he exclaimed proudly.

Norman felt movement at the foot of his bed. Snuggled up, with his paw over his nose, lay Morph. Lazily, he uncurled himself, stood and stretched his back to that almost impossible angle that cats somehow manage and sat looking around the room.

Whilst Norman and the round-faced man returned his gaze, to the absolute amazement of Norman, Morph spoke. It was a clear, educated voice that exuded authority, even though it only consisted of a single word.

"Chicken."

Morph appeared just as surprised as Norman with his outburst, but it was followed with an expression of smugness.

"This is most irregular," the man cried. "Somehow, when you died, you and your cat were fused together. Normally, it is just a select few who are lucky enough to make it to our centre, but in your case—" he looked at Norman. "It appears you have a companion."

Chapter 3

The Classroom

Shortly after their awakening, introductions were made and Norman discovered the genial man was named Abathar.

"My official title is The Weigher of Souls."

Norman pulled a face.

"Yes, I know it is rather dramatic, so instead I go by The Purveyor of Opportunistic Power. . . or Sir Poop for short."

Norman and Morph followed Sir Poop out of the bedroom and down a very long, brightly-lit corridor with a solid-looking red door at the end. The silence in the corridor was almost deafening and even Morph's fur bristled at the eeriness of the situation they found themselves in.

Suspended on one of the walls were small portraits of important-looking people—Elizabeth Fry, Sir Isaac Newton, Queen Elizabeth I, Leonardo Da Vinci, Sir Tim Berners-Lee, Professor Brian Cox and many more outstanding figures of humanity, going back many centuries.

Norman paused briefly at each picture and read the nameplate with interest, trying to recall their achievements from BBC documentaries that his parents made him watch when he was younger.

Sir Poop stopped outside a light blue door half-way down the corridor. Fixed above the entrance was a small plastic plaque that read, 'Training Room 834.'

Next to the door dangled a picture of Albert Einstein, posing with his trademark pipe and wild grey hair. Inscribed below the picture were the words, 'Albert. Saved by Lord Bruce III.'

Sir Poop opened the door, flipped on the light switch and a few seconds later strobe lights flickered into life, revealing a square room with a large, well-worn desk and a clean white board at the front. Facing the board and the desk were four tables set out in the classic 1940s classroom style.

Sir Poop invited Norman and Morph to take a seat and strode purposely to the front of the class.

"Right. Let's get started," Sir Poop said, pausing for dramatic effect, whilst Norman took his seat. Morph sprang lightly from the floor up to the seat next to him.

"As I'm sure you are aware by now, you are both dead."

Not the most uplifting start to a class, Norman thought, but he forced himself to remain silent.

"However," Sir Poop continued with gusto. "You have been specially selected to become a Ghosteleer, which is one of the highest honours one can achieve after death. A Ghosteleer's mission is to protect human beings who are destined to become great inventors or make discoveries that will improve the living world. The pictures you saw hanging in the corridor outside are examples of some of our finest work. If it were not for our brave Ghosteleers, humans would never have progressed and would most likely be extinct now, like the dinosaurs, who unfortunately did not employ our protection services.

"After five years' service as a Ghosteleer, you will painlessly dissolve and head into the light to a beautiful paradise where you can remain in peace for the rest of existence."

Norman, unable to restrain himself any longer, excitedly put up his hand.

"Excuse me Sir Poop, but do you mean Heaven?"

"Actually, it's more like Brighton. May I carry on?"

Without waiting for an answer, Sir Poop continued his lecture with such enthusiasm Norman thought he might burst like an over-inflated balloon.

"Only a very small number of individuals are lucky enough to be chosen as a Ghosteleer and receive the special powers that go with the job. When you die, we take different aspects of your body, mind and soul and increase their ability. Your brain, for example, is sharpened like a razor so it can react to and overcome any tricky situation it faces."

Norman, whose attention had now piqued, sat up straight in his uncomfortable chair.

"I've become more intelligent," he mused with a satisfied look.

He tried to think of something smart that he would have found impossible before he died. He decided on naming all the planets in the solar system.

"Mercury, Venus, Earth, Mars, Jupiter, Saturn. . ." he paused, concentrating on what could be next.

Meanwhile, Sir Poop—now in full swing—exuberantly listed all the parts of Norman and Morph that had been honed like a finely tuned instrument.

"Your legs will never tire; your minds will be able to lift heavy objects and your hair will never go grey. However, the part of you that is the most significant and I'm most proud of is—"

"Uranus!" Morph erupted. "For goodness sake Norman, it's Uranus!"

Stunned silence descended in the room.

"I can hear every word you say in your mind and it's making the fur on the back of my neck stand on end. It's like an infestation of mice that I can't pounce upon. I'm a cat. I used to sleep and eat chicken! It's true, I occasionally pooed in the front garden and blamed it on Socksy next door; but that was my life and I loved it. Now, I must live the next five years with your thoughts in my mind, and the worst thing is you didn't feed me before you selfishly blew us up, so I'll always be hungry! AAARGH!"

Morph hissed, twitched his long whiskers and skulked off, with his tail between his legs, to sit at the back of the classroom.

"Well," continued Sir Poop. "I was going to say your ears."

Several minutes later the tension in the room had eased a little and Sir Poop went on to explain that Ghosteleers don't sleep, eat anything (including chicken), or go to the toilet. Ever.

Norman could hear a continuous 'thump' at the back of the classroom as Morph banged his head against the desk, presumably in despair that his purpose as a cat had evaporated.

Chapter 4

The Test

For the next two days, Norman and Morph were placed in separate classrooms, each with a severe-looking teacher determined to understand their pupil's potential. The rooms were almost identical to the one that Sir Poop had first taken them to—a windowless shell with a few abstract pictures dotted around, not dissimilar to a doctor's waiting room.

Situated at the back of Norman's room was something like a child's play area with dozens of wooden bricks strewn across a table, giving the impression that a small explosion had occurred in the previous class.

Norman's teacher, Asmodel, strolled purposefully towards the rear table and sat down with authority on an aged, dark, wooden stool. His black hair was immaculately groomed and his white shirt looked like it had been ironed only a few seconds earlier. He wore light grey, pressed trousers, held up with a brown belt and buckle that sparkled in the overhead spotlights. His black leather shoes gleamed as if they had never been worn before that day.

Asmodel invited Norman to sit on the opposite chair.

"I'm going to teach you everything you need to become a great Ghosteleer. One of your new powers—actually it is my favourite—is telekinesis."

Norman didn't know what telekinesis was, but he guessed that it was something to do with television and stiff knees. All of which he had experienced in the past whilst lying next to the wood-burning stove watching *The X Factor* with Morph.

"How does losing the feeling in my legs help me?" Norman questioned.

Asmodel smiled gently. "Telekinesis is the ability to move objects with your mind. Let's take this wooden brick here." He lifted a well-worn, smooth-edged, apple-sized block to the front of the table. "I would like you to focus your inner soul and project an imaginary beam from your mind to the brick and force it to move across the table."

Norman suppressed a little smirk that contained more than a fair share of scepticism, until Asmodel looked squarely at the brick, and a second later it slid effortlessly across the desk and fell neatly into Norman's lap.

Stunned, Norman examined the brick in minute detail looking for ball-bearings, wheels, magnets, or anything that could rationally explain the magic he had just witnessed.

"Go on, give it a go. It only takes new Ghosteleers a few minutes to master this simple task."

Norman placed the brick on the table in front of him and stared hard at it. Nothing happened. He squinted and gave the block the full might of his gaze. Still nothing happened.

"Focus your soul. Use your brain to reach out to the block and push it across the desk," Asmodel encouraged.

Norman squeezed, pushed, pulled and pressed what he thought was his soul until his face went red and he let out a fart that embarrassingly echoed around the room.

Asmodel shifted uncomfortably in his seat and politely pretended not to hear it.

Three hours and twenty minutes later, Asmodel decided a short break was in order. After six hours, a longer break was required.

On day three, Asmodel's hair resembled a bird's nest. Beads of sweat covered his brow, borne out of frustration and anger. The patience he had shown at the beginning of their session was no more than a distant memory, long buried under a tortuous few days with Norman.

He stood, slightly shaking, and trembled across the room towards the door like a man who had turned one hundred years old and suddenly lost the will to live.

Just then the wooden block facing Norman twitched and shuddered, as if it had been given the kiss of life. Although it only moved about a centimetre, Norman felt like it had flown across a continent. He spun on his stool and faced the quaking Asmodel with a satisfied grin that stretched from ear to ear.

"What's next?" Norman smugly enquired.

Asmodel stopped, turned, shook his head and shuffled slowly out of the door, mumbling as he went.

*

Sometime later, a new teacher appeared in the doorway and introduced herself as Tabris. Apparently Asmodel had been reassigned.

Norman stared in wonder at Tabris and instantly fell in love with her pony-tailed, glossy, dark hair, wide intelligent eyes and slim athletic figure.

Tabris, on the other hand, knew that she had a challenge on her hands in bringing Norman up to the same standard as the other cadets. He would be meeting them all in a short while.

Wanting to impress his new teacher, Norman tried particularly hard over the next few days and eventually managed to move the stubborn wooden block from one side of the table to the other, without releasing any trapped wind. He'd been particularly proud of this achievement and hoped that Tabris felt the same way.

To Norman's relief and pleasure, Tabris suggested that they meet up with Morph, who had been studiously learning in the classroom adjacent to theirs.

As they ambled to the door, Norman couldn't help but be pleased with his performance since Asmodel had left the classroom and was eager to share his success with Morph.

Tabris turned the handle on the classroom door. Norman froze in mid-walk. His face transformed from a look of self-satisfaction to one that had been slapped with a large plank of wood. . . with a wet fish attached for good measure.

At the front of the class, Morph was sitting on a stool, deep in conversation with Sir Poop, whilst dozens of wooden blocks floated effortlessly in a synchronised dance above the table. At ten-second intervals, the letters on the side of the blocks spelled the word 'chicken.' Just as a conductor swirls his baton at an orchestra, Morph's tail appeared to be directing the blocks with elegant, fluid swishes.

"So according to Newton's second law of motion, the acceleration of an object as produced by a net force is directly proportional to the magnitude of the net force, in the same direction as the net force, and inversely proportional to the mass of the object," Morph clarified. "Well, that explains why I was unable to move the entire building then."

"Exactly!" beamed Sir Poop. "I was fortunate enough to have Newton himself explain it to me."

At that moment, Sir Poop glanced up and looked warmly upon Norman and Tabris, who were invited to sit down next to them. Sir Poop cleared his throat.

"The initial training and testing phase is now complete and I can share the results with you." Sir Poop turned and fired a steely gaze in Norman's direction.

Norman felt his stomach turn with a mixture of fear and impending disappointment. He recalled a similar conversation with his maths teacher in secondary school.

"You have no doubt heard of the eighty-twenty rule?" Sir Poop asked.

Norman nodded. He knew from the display above

Morph's table that it was himself who was likely to have twenty per cent ability, whilst Morph was the eighty per cent in that rule. He could almost feel himself give a grudgingly accepting shrug at the prospect.

"Well, this is more of a ninety-five-five rule," Sir Poop said.

Norman let out an exasperated breath. In school, he'd been used to being out-performed by the whole class, with the exception of Rocco, whom, in an attempt to prove how tough he was, had decided to run head first into an oak tree at the age of nine. Unfortunately, the tree won on that occasion. Since that moment, Rocco had been unable to recall any lesson from the moment he walked out of the classroom door. Now, all these years later, Norman's own cat was proving himself more intelligent than him!

Morph looked at his owner with an expression of sympathy, which made Norman feel even more depressed, especially after being used to the 'hungry' look he'd received in the years up to that point.

"There is, however, an interesting twist," Sir Poop said. "Although Morph has some of the most impressive powers ever seen in the history of Ghosteleers, his strength weakens the further away he is from you, Norman. Something to do with the fusion at the time of your death, I would imagine. Therefore, you will be our first Ghosteleer partnership. Congratulations! You can now proceed to the next level. But first, I think you both deserve a little break. Let me show you around our facility and I'll introduce you to a few of our other cadets. Some of whom are rather special."

Chapter 5

The Others

Abathar exited the room, with Norman and Morph behind him and they headed for the bright red door at the end of the corridor that the newcomers had first noticed on their arrival.

Tabris stood to one side to let them pass and then closed the classroom door gently behind her. She had a bright, excited look in her eyes.

Morph trotted alongside Sir Poop, eager to explore somewhere other than the classrooms. It appeared that his natural curiosity had not diminished since he had passed away.

Positioned next to the door—fastened to the wall—lay a matt, black square in which Sir Poop now placed his hand. A blue flash scanned his stubby fingers and sweaty palm. Immediately, a loud click could be heard followed by Sir Poop gripping the vertical handle and opening the door wide to allow Morph, Norman and Tabris through.

The sound from the hall struck Morph and Norman like a cannon ball. It wasn't a threatening noise, but after the quiet solitude of training within the classroom, it reminded Norman of the week before Christmas during rush hour at Victoria station in London. Morph edged a little closer to Norman.

A giant dome towered above them, filled with hundreds of people of all races, shapes and sizes.

A gigantic wrestler with tanned skin ambled past wearing nothing but his star-spangled pants, knee-length white socks and glittery red boots. He slapped Sir Poop heavily on the back and offered a friendly greeting of, "Yo, it's the Poopmeister!"

Sir Poop regained his balance, smiled politely and swiftly moved on.

Gliding across the room from the opposite direction came a beautiful, dark-skinned woman wearing a brightly coloured dress complemented by three or four silk scarves. The trail of the scarves floated effortlessly above the marble floor as if an invisible child was holding them up.

Sir Poop bowed his head and acknowledged her as, "Your Majesty." She returned his salutation with a kind smile and continued to make her way towards a group of serious-looking individuals at the far edge of the room.

To the right of Tabris, two sporty, young, Oriental ladies were playing table tennis. One of the players was dressed in black tracksuit bottoms and a blue t-shirt. She served the ball to her opponent who flicked it back at speed to the other side of the table. In a split second, the ball returned over the net having been swiped by a floating bat next to the first player.

Norman noticed a similar floating bat on the other side of the table, making up an unusual doubles partnership. In between shots, the two bats floated a metre off the ground and bobbed up and down like corks in a bath.

Just then the woman in the blue t-shirt smashed the ball ferociously on to the opponent's half of the table, which caused the floating bat to scurry back some distance in a desperate attempt to hit the ball. Unfortunately, it only succeeded in striking the bottom of an un-amused, angry, small man with a bowler hat who was passing nearby.

Norman and Morph stood motionless in the middle of the dome and turned slowly, taking in the marvellous variety of sights and sounds that surrounded them. The assembled crowd were not too dissimilar to a fancy-dress party at the United Nations.

After several minutes absorbing the spectacle, Morph sauntered towards a table in which two smartly dressed men were engaged in a game of chess. Unusually, the chess board floated in mid-air between the two whilst gracefully rotating in neat circles.

As the players gazed up, the board flipped over revealing a second game of chess underneath. Just then a knight moved across the board and took a bishop, which fluttered gently down to the table like a feather in a summer breeze.

"Excellent move, Silas," Sir Poop said. "May I interrupt your game to introduce our latest Ghosteleer recruits?" After a few seconds' pause, whilst Sir Poop waited for some kind of recognition that didn't come, he said. "This is Norman and his cat Morph."

Silas, clearly irritated at being disturbed during his games, locked eyes with Norman and offered a slight inclination of the head in a lukewarm welcome. He then turned to Morph and sarcastically muttered, "What an adorable cat," before returning his focus to the games in hand.

Morph bristled and extended his claws so that they scratched the polished floor. He retorted with an equally sarcastic, "Why, thank you very much, but I do think queen to knight four would have been a much more effective move," before the board came crashing down to the table.

"You ruined my game, cat," said Silas in a menacingly slow drawl.

He stood up and towered over Morph. This drew the attention of several others who clustered around Morph and Norman for a better look at the newcomers.

Morph stared alarmingly upwards as the swarm of legs drew threateningly closer, appearing as a circular tower of limbs.

Norman, oblivious to his cat's concern, suddenly heard a voice echo inside his head, *Pick me up, now!*

Norman's first reaction had been to look around to see who had spoken, but he felt sure that the voice resounded only in his head. He then looked down at Morph, who returned his gaze with pleading eyes, as more legs started jostling closer.

The voice in Norman's head then spoke again. *Hurry!*

In an instant, Norman swiftly picked up Morph and cradled him close to his chest.

It was the first time he had ever heard another voice inside his head other than his own, but it felt strangely comforting knowing that he had a constant companion. Having now been picked up, Morph purred a little with gratitude and snuggled closer to Norman.

After several minutes, Sir Poop settled the curious crowd and escorted Norman and Morph to a quieter area within the dome, much to their relief.

"This is the main meeting place for all the Ghosteleers and staff," Tabris explained. "It does get pretty loud. Mainly because time doesn't exist, so no-one gets tired, hungry or needs the loo, there is always a constant buzz in here."

She then started walking towards a pastel green door.

As they entered the adjoining room, Norman gently lowered Morph to the floor and gazed around in wonder. Tall trees and plush bushes encircled them, whilst golden-paved paths intriguingly intertwined, flowing through the shrubbery like meandering streams.

Sir Poop took a step forward and spoke quietly. "You may well have guessed; this is the Garden Room. Each path leads to a central fountain where you can contemplate your thoughts and have a little quiet time. I ask that you respect other people's serenity whilst you are in here."

Norman stole another glance at Tabris, who lingered at the back of the room, and noticed how peaceful and content she looked. Even Norman could tell that this sanctuary had special meaning to her.

"There are two other doors on your left, over there. One is the Forest Room and the other is the Stream Room. I would recommend any of these locations to enhance your skills over the coming days. They are peaceful and surprisingly spacious. Just don't get lost."

Just then the door opened and a giggling couple around Norman's age entered the room. They greeted Sir Poop with a cheery, "Hello," followed by a warm, "Hi Tabris."

Tabris gave the newcomers a kiss on the cheek and introduced them as Nick and Lynn, who, it turned out, had arrived as Ghosteleers six months earlier.

After a few minutes of small talk—consisting of which humans they had saved in the past few weeks—Nick and Lynn offered to show Norman and Morph around the facility. They appeared to accept Morph's abilities much better than the group in the main dome.

Sir Poop reluctantly agreed to leave Norman and Morph with Nick and Lynn, remembering that he had to prepare some documents for the visit of the President of the Facility in two weeks' time. Both he and Tabris headed off to the main dome.

"It's pretty difficult adjusting when you first arrive, what with no sleep, no sense of time, no food and all that," Nick said. "Sir Poop is good at testing you and making sure your skills are developed, but when it comes to explaining what on earth is going on, he falls a bit short."

To Norman, Nick had summed up exactly how he'd felt since waking up as a Ghosteleer. Morph too seemed very interested in the different perspective that Nick and Lynn could offer.

Lynn opened the door marked Stream Room and headed through, followed closely by Nick, Norman and Morph. It felt as if they had been transported into another world, as Norman observed a babbling brook flowing effortlessly through dark green swaying grass. High above them, wisps of clouds floated through a perfect blue sky.

"The sky is all computer generated, even the breeze," Nick explained. "Everything else is real though, including the mosquitos. I have no idea why they included them."

Every so often, a small stone bridge would appear, allowing the casual stroller to explore deeper into the landscape. After several minutes of pleasant ambling, the group rested on a large, curved, wooden bench that miraculously seemed to appear out of nowhere.

Norman decided that he liked his new companions and thought it to be a good time to quiz them on their experiences as Ghosteleers.

Lynn spun on her seat and gazed intently at Norman and Morph. She then purposefully slid her shirt sleeve up her wrist until it revealed what looked initially like a watch, but without any hands or obvious display.

"This is the Messenger," Lynn clarified, as she motioned towards the device. "Once you have passed your exams, you will receive one. Every Messenger is unique and programmed to its paired Ghosteleer. You can never take it off until your final assignment has been completed."

"But, what does it do?" questioned Morph.

"If it starts flashing green, you have an assignment waiting," Nick explained. "When that happens, you need to make your way as quickly as possible to Potts' laboratory —he's the Portal Engineer—where you will be given your briefing. This includes the background on the human you need to save and what they can do in the future. After the briefing, Potts will escort you through the Portal."

Norman looked at Morph who appeared transfixed whilst his tail swished excitedly over the edge of the bench.

"Once you have stepped through the Portal, your Messenger will appear red and count down from sixty minutes. You have exactly that amount of time to save your human from the Horags," Nick said.

"The what?" Norman exclaimed, looking a little flustered.

"The Horags. They are the opposite of us. Their main purpose is to stop humans inventing, improving, creating or developing in the world. They particularly don't like people who find new ways to cure diseases. The more important the human, the stronger the Horag that is sent to try and finish them off. We're only new, so we've only come across weak Horags so far, but they're definitely getting tougher," Lynn said.

Morph noticed that Norman's face had drained of all colour but decided to continue his questioning. "So, do we actually have to fight these Horags to save the human?"

"Not physically, no. It's like a game of chess, with the human being the king. If the king is threatened by the Horag, then you move them to safety or put something in the Horag's path to block the danger. If the human is still alive at the end of sixty minutes, then you win and humanity benefits from their creation. However, if the Horag manages to get to the human. . . well, no benefit to humankind and no human either."

An involuntary shudder passed through Norman as the last of the colour faded miserably from his already pale face. He'd never been responsible for another human in his life and now that he was dead, he would have to bear the weight of another person's life on his shoulders.

He glanced at Morph hoping to see a similar reaction of shock in his bright eyes, but instead noticed that his whiskers were twitching and his tail was swooshing in obvious excitement.

"A real life—or dead—version of cat and mouse. How purrrfect!"

Chapter 6

The Laboratory

After several hours of gentle strolling through the rooms around the facility, Norman's composure had returned a little and so had the colour to his face. The knowledge that he had the support of his new friends—and Morph—provided him with a well-needed comfort boost.

Continuing their journey, the small group explored the library, which was filled from floor to ceiling with thousands of leather-bound books, and the movie room that contained the very latest films. Apparently watching *Harry Potter* was compulsory, as it made you a more effective Ghosteleer. Norman, having seen each film twice, felt much more reassured.

Nick eventually steered them towards a large set of high-security double doors, just off from the main hall, that they had seen when they had first arrived.

A highly-polished metal sign was screwed to the wall

to the left of the door. Etched on it in capital letters were the words, THE PORTAL, followed by smaller words underneath that read, cared for by Finley Potts.

Nick rapped on the door, looked up to the myriad security cameras, placed his hand on a scanner attached to the wall and then pushed the door lightly forward. It swung noiselessly open and Nick confidently strolled through, followed by Lynn, Norman and then Morph.

In the far corner of the room, a small man with wide-rimmed spectacles and an oil-stained apron stood up, whilst holding a large screwdriver. A smile instantly beamed across his face as he made his way towards Nick.

"Nick, great to see you again. Hi Lynn, how are you?" He had a clear, animated voice that was both reassuring and soothing.

"I'm fine, thanks," Lynn replied warmly. "We've come to introduce you to our new friends Norman and Morph. And this—" she said, motioning towards the energetic character. "Is the best portal engineer of all time, Potts."

Norman and Potts shook hands and then Potts turned his attention to Morph.

"Ah, I've heard a great deal about you, Morph. It's been so long since I've seen a cat, let alone a Devonshire Rex. I must say your coat is absolutely beautiful. May I?"

He stretched out his small hand and gently stroked Morph behind his ear. To the surprise of everyone in the group, Morph purred loudly and closed his eyes in delight.

Norman took this opportunity to observe the brightly lit room, which felt like a futuristic workshop. At one end of the room, he noticed a series of wooden pegs secured to the wall, each holding a Messenger device like the one Lynn had shown them earlier. Above these, fastened to the ceiling, hung a giant screen not dissimilar to those displayed in railway stations. At least twenty names were emblazoned in big bold lettering across the glossy screen, with a number next to each name. It reminded Norman of his local Argos store back home. At the very top of the list, Norman noticed Silas's name with sixty-one next to it.

Potts followed Norman's gaze and looked up at the screen.

"The leader board shows us who the best performing Ghosteleers are, and at the end of each year, the winner has their name chiselled into a stone plaque, which is then hung in the main hall. Silas has won it every season since he arrived and with a score of sixty-one, I don't think anyone is going to catch him. Sixty-one is the total number of lives he has saved this year. Pretty impressive stuff."

Morph, who had now recovered from his fussing, noticed that the next closest person had a score of forty-two with the remaining Ghosteleers all appearing to be within ten points of each other. Lynn's name appeared in fourth position with a score of thirty-nine.

"Anything over twenty-five is deemed to be rather good," Potts assured. "Here, let me show you the Portal."

Norman and Morph followed the excited Potts across to the far side of the workshop where a giant, metallic, silver arch stood gleaming under several spotlights. Hundreds of cables flowed around the outside to various points in the room, spreading like roots from a tree. A light, transparent, blue film formed the entrance to the arch, which moved fluidly in the same way as bubble blowing mixture.

A gentle hum emanated from the structure, which Potts proudly rubbed with a rag he had taken from his apron pocket.

The circular arch stood ten feet tall and dominated the corner of the room. Positioned just to the left of the Portal stood a curved control panel with more switches, lights and levers than Norman had ever seen.

"Pick me up," Morph said to Norman. Morph was amazed by the technology and wanted to get a closer look.

"It appears to be a particle accelerator that manipulates electromagnetic fields to propel Ghosteleers through space time at near light speed. Is that an accurate supposition?" Morph asked.

The smile that spread across Potts' face couldn't have been wider. His enthusiasm was positively brimming now.

"Exactly! There is a significant amount of quantum mechanics involved. I had some difficulty with the probability densities of wave functions, but I managed to resolve it after playing with a box of Maltesers. It struck me there was a distinct similarity between the Maltesers and the way electrons perform in a hydrogen atom. It was just a shame I couldn't eat them afterwards," Potts wistfully added.

Norman didn't even pretend to understand the conversation between Potts and Morph, except for the bit about playing with Maltesers, so he decided to have a closer look at the arch containing the blue fluid film.

The swirling motion, in what looked like bubble mixture,

produced an almost hypnotic effect on him. He advanced to within a few centimetres and stared hard at the substance. As he did so, a face suddenly appeared on the other side of the film that rapidly moved towards him with such speed, their heads bumped into each other with a deep thudding sound.

A terrified Norman flew back and went crashing into Lynn, who in turn fell upon Nick. Nick stumbled and stepped on to Potts' foot, who instinctively threw Morph into the air as he tried to regain his balance.

Morph, now airborne, stretched out his paws and landed deftly on top of the control panel, which instantly beeped in alarm. The electric hum of the machinery died away, the lights dimmed and an eerie silence descended upon the room followed by a distinct burning smell.

A few seconds later, the quietness ended abruptly when a strange woman holding her head let out a tirade of rude words, most of which Norman had never heard before. Potts rushed to her side in a brave attempt to appease her.

"Who's this bloomin' bampot?" she railed in a broad Scottish accent, whilst gesturing towards Norman.

Norman continued to stand with his mouth agape, still rubbing his bruised head, uncertain how best to pacify the angry woman with wild hair that stood like a monolith in front of him.

Luckily, Potts came to his rescue.

"Maudie, these are our new arrivals, Norman and Morph. How are you feeling now? Are you hurt? You know when the power gets cut off within the Portal it's like a guillotine that can literally slice you in half. You were very lucky to escape unscathed."

"No thanks to you," came the terse reply aimed at Norman, with a stare that could freeze water. "If I'm going to get chopped in half, it's going to take more than this wee numpty to do it. Just remember this. I am the toughest Ghosteleer there is and my reputation is as fierce as my fists. Nobody ever makes a fool out of Mad Maudie, so keep your bumbling ways far away from me."

She flung her head high and turned to the exit. Only then did the group observe that the hair on the back of her head was singed and lightly smoking, with a large clump missing.

As Norman lowered his gaze, he noticed that Mad Maudie's bottom was poking through what used to be a high-quality woollen skirt. It appeared the guillotine had cut a closer shave than she thought.

"And Potts, get this room sorted out! It stinks of burning and there is a terrible draught coming from somewhere."

Nobody said a word as the bare bottomed Maudie briskly closed the door behind her and headed for the communal hall.

Chapter 7

The Teacher

Potts soon restored the power and the gentle thumping whirr of the machinery started again, returning life to the metallic Portal. The new friends said their goodbyes, promising to catch up again later.

Norman and Morph decided to head back to the Stream Room, whilst Nick and Lynn opted for a game of hands-free table football.

The sunlight still flowed brightly across the glade, warming the fur on Morph's back. He stretched his front paws forward into the soft grass, arched his back high into the air and sat upright, curling his tail around so that it covered his paws.

"Norman, I'm going to teach you how to listen to my thoughts. I've figured out how to open and block your mind—thank goodness! I believe it would be an advantage to us if you could reciprocate, so that you can hear what I'm thinking. There may be times in the future when it's best we communicate without speaking. Open your mind like a tap and just let the thoughts fall through. Let's try words with one syllable for now. How about cat?"

The two companions continued to practice as the sun curled across the pale blue sky. Eventually, after many failed attempts, a glimmer of hope appeared on the horizon.

"Okay, Norman. I'm going to think of something and I want you to say my thought out loud."

Morph closed his eyes tightly in fierce concentration and willed the word 'chicken' over to Norman's mind, eager for him to reach out and grasp it. He knew he had to encourage Norman to search for thoughts, rather than have them rammed into his consciousness.

"I have it! I have it! The word you are thinking of is chicken! Am I right?"

"Correct! Well done, that's excellent. We'll need to keep training though."

Just then, a rustling sound came from their left and Tabris approached along the gravel pathway. Norman admired her sparkling eyes and the flow of her hair as she strolled towards them. He felt his heart race a little bit faster in the anticipation of her company.

"Well, I'm definitely turning off your thoughts now," murmured Morph.

"Do you mind if I join you?" Tabris asked.

"Not at all. Morph was just teaching me to—"

"Move some pebbles," Morph quickly interjected and threw Norman a look as if to say, 'Let's keep this to ourselves.'

By now the sun had dipped low over the trees, producing a golden glow that reflected beautifully off the stream.

As the three of them lay on the grass, Norman spoke of their visit to Potts' Portal Room and even recounted the confrontation with Maudie and her bare behind. They all laughed so hard that tears flowed from Tabris' eyes, which made them laugh even more.

It was at that moment that Tabris realised how different Norman was to everyone else in the facility. He wasn't strong, ruthless, intelligent or even particularly good looking, but he did have a kindness entwined in his soul that she warmed to.

The group continued chatting for some time, when the subject of the Horags came up. Tabris explained that even in the afterlife, there needs to be a balance between good and evil.

"The Horags are a wicked group that will do their best to destroy the humans that the Ghosteleers are assigned to protect. Their leader is the merciless Apollyon, although nobody has seen him in centuries. Legend goes that his pointed finger nails are poisonous, and a single scrape will banish a Ghosteleer to Skegness for all eternity. It is said that Apollyon enjoys nothing more than ripping apart a soul and watching it float endlessly in pieces around the Skeggy ether. There's only one Ghosteleer who would ever be brave enough to face Apollyon and that is Ms Thorne, the President of the Ghosteleers."

As Tabris elaborated, she spoke of Ms Thorne's severe

reputation. Firstly, as the greatest, most revered Ghosteleer to have ever stepped through the Portal. Secondly, as the most pugnacious President that the organisation has ever had. She would constantly battle the afterlife Council for extra funding to enable her Ghosteleer empire to flourish and grow. It took an extremely brave—or very stupid—individual to offer an opinion that didn't align with hers.

"I think I'm going to be sick. Where's the toilet?" asked Norman, clearly taken aback by these latest revelations.

Morph shook his head and Tabris simply smiled.

"There are no toilets, silly! Remember? No food, no drink, no sleeping, no toilets? Okay, how about something more cheerful. I'm going to be your teacher and the lessons start now."

The mood certainly became more upbeat as they practised moving different objects using only their minds. Even Norman managed to lift a smooth grey pebble from the shallow stream so that it spun freely above the water.

They honed their Ghosteleer skills and watched as darkness fell upon the Stream Room, causing long shadows to reach out over the lush green grass.

Tabris decided they deserved a break, so they headed towards the exit.

The next lesson would take place in Room 306 in a couple of hours.

*

The lesson resumed in the more formal setting of a classroom that Norman and Morph had not seen before. Although the room appeared smaller than the one they had been in with Sir Poop, the walls were painted a sunshine yellow, giving it a bright, spacious feel.

Tabris, cradling a marker pen, stood at the front of the class next to a well-used white board that had several messages drawn on it in very neat handwriting. She pointed to the top line and read through each sentence systematically.

After the last instruction, Norman understood that once you pass through the Portal, you have sixty minutes to find your human and save them from harm. The Messenger device will start counting down the second you step into the human world. When there is one minute remaining, you press the button on the Messenger and the Portal will re-appear. If you fail to enter the Portal within the allocated time, you will evaporate and no longer exist in any form.

"The golden rule that both Ghosteleers and Horags must observe is that at no point can you use your telepathy skills to directly move a human. People can never see us, but on some occasions an individual can be possessed by a Horag and controlled to do harm to others."

Norman thought back to occasions in his life when he'd been driving and suddenly become aware of his surroundings but couldn't remember getting there. Tabris explained that a Horag could have taken control of him and a Ghosteleer might have prevented a special human stepping out in front of his car. A chill descended Norman's spine as Tabris continued her teaching.

"Always attempt to move your human away from cars. Sixty-five percent of road accidents occur because of poor driver reactions, so this makes it a perfect environment for Horags to prey upon people. Also, stay clear of sheds and the kitchen. . . and cows," she added as a whimsical afterthought.

Norman and Morph each threw a quizzical look at Tabris, who felt obliged to explain her choice of words.

"It happened not so long ago, just before I had been asked to become a teacher. I entered the Portal, as I had done hundreds of times before, and found myself in a remote open area somewhere in Brazil during the early hours of the morning. José Martinez was my assigned human and he was a world expert in mobile network technology. I assume you've heard of 3G and 4G phone networks? Well, he had in his sights a vision of 11G networks that could transmit taste and smell.

"I found his old farmhouse easily enough, built into the side of a steep hillside and surrounded only by alpacas and cows. José and his wife were fast asleep in bed, so I decided to do a safety check on the building. I checked his slippers for the lethal Brazilian wandering spider, went into the bathroom to make sure no water had spilt onto the slippery tiles and I checked the locks on every window and door. It seemed safe. He couldn't possibly be hurt."

Tabris paused, took a deep breath and then continued, "But I underestimated the Horag. The cunning little monster roamed outside in the moonlight using his telekinesis powers to control a large branch that he'd found on the floor. He used the stick to direct a cow up the steep slope behind the house and on to the roof of the house. Before I knew what was happening, the slates gave way and a surprised cow fell right on top of José, flattening him like a pancake. I didn't see that one coming, I can tell you."

Chapter 8

The Return to Potts

The lessons continued in rapid succession, teaching everything from following a human to the venomous snakes of west Africa. Norman felt like his brain was a sponge. Not because it absorbed large amounts of information, but simply because it contained lots of holes and not much ability.

Eventually, Tabris called time on the classroom and declared that they would pay a visit to the human world for a hands-on battle with a Horag. Morph twitched his whiskers, perked his ears and eagerly followed Tabris out of the door and down the long corridor towards the bustling communal hall.

In every direction, people were scurrying around, playing games or conversing in an animated fashion. Morph noticed Silas at the edge of the room, participating in what appeared to be a very serious discussion with a heavily tattooed man in a long, flowing, burgundy cloak. Whatever they were debating, it appeared that Silas didn't want to be overheard. In the next moment, he gripped the man by the arm and ushered him to one of the quieter rooms off the main hall.

Norman picked up Morph, without being asked to do so, and criss-crossed the room, following Tabris as best he could. She glided effortlessly through the swarm of people, knowing instinctively the easiest route to take. Several minutes later, they arrived at the Portal's high-security double doors and Norman released Morph who landed gently on the ground.

In addition to the multiple cameras and high-tech security equipment that Norman recognised from their previous visit, there now appeared to be a newly installed cat-flap.

Tabris gawped in disbelief, shaking her head slowly as she did so. Printed on the front of the flap in large bold letters were the words,

ONLY FOR USE BY MORPH

Tabris wondered whether someone else might try and fit through the opening if the notice wasn't there.

By the time Tabris had scanned her hand and performed the other necessary authentication checks, a very smug Morph was sitting with Potts, thanking him for the delightful new purpose-built entrance.

As they exchanged pleasantries, Norman could feel the gentle humming of the machinery reverberating around the room. The portal still contained the entrancing swirling motion within its arched frame.

Several minutes later, Tabris turned her attention to the mission in hand. "Potts, I would like to take Norman and Morph on an assignment somewhere nice and quiet. Do you think you could find a suitable human for me please?"

"Of course! Let me look through my data bank."

Potts enthusiastically shuffled off to the main control panel and started pressing buttons and pulling levers until an image of a human appeared on the large TV screen above them.

The picture revealed a teenage boy with a mop of bright orange hair sprouting from a large forehead like an erupting volcano. Underneath his large spectacles, a cheeky grin stretched from ear to ear, whilst a million freckles adorned the rest of his pale face.

"This is Shaun Mathewson, aged seventeen from Los Angeles. He will go on to create the fastest re-filling toilet mankind has ever known. Not sure why he looks so wishy-washy, when he should appear *flushed*."

Tabris groaned at Potts' attempt at toilet humour, wondering which Christmas cracker that had come from.

"Your meeting point will be on the outskirts of the city at Eldred Street. The neighbourhood is pretty sparse, and the time of day is seven in the morning. There are very few people around. Should be an absolute doddle for a seasoned expert such as you, Tabris."

"Perfect! Norman, Morph, let's go kick some Horag butt."

Even though Tabris jovially spoke in a very exaggerated American accent, Norman still felt the gravity of the situation and knew that Shaun's life was precariously balanced in their hands.

Potts strode purposefully to the Messenger devices hanging on the wall and returned with a pink plastic bracelet for Norman, marked 'Trainee,' and a beautiful golden collar adorned with diamond clusters for Morph, which he gently attached after receiving an approving nod.

After the Messengers had been comfortably fitted, Potts reached for a device hanging from a hook next to the control panel. To Morph, it appeared to be a highly-sophisticated piece of spherical technology that would wirelessly transmit a short-range signal to a receiver. To Norman, it looked like a doughnut on a stick.

"This is my Wave Over Messenger Bluetooth Link Extension, or WOMBLE. With it I can activate the Messenger and set the time you spend in the human world. The default is sixty minutes, but in exceptional circumstances it can be different."

Potts waved the WOMBLE over Morph's collar. A second later, a high-pitched beep could be heard as the Messenger registered the allocated time. Norman and Tabris had their Messengers set immediately after, each producing an identical sound.

"Okay, you're all set. The hour will begin the moment you step through the Portal. When you have a minute left, the Messenger will sound an alarm and count down. You then have sixty seconds to press the button on the side of the Messenger to reactivate the Portal and safely return. If you leave it any later, you won't return."

Tabris clapped her hands in excitement and marched towards the Portal. Norman and Morph hesitantly followed.

"Follow me," Tabris said.

She stepped into the twirling Portal and dissolved into thin air. A few seconds later, Morph gingerly walked through with his tail almost dragging on the ground.

Norman held his breath as if he were jumping into an infinity swimming pool and forced his feet to move forward. As his fingers reached out and touched the Portal, a strange tickling sensation flooded through his arm. He immediately retracted his hand in alarm and wondered how he could escape this madness.

Potts, who was now behind the control panel, raised his hands in a shooing motion, ignoring Norman's pleading eyes and beckoned him to go through the archway.

Frozen to the spot, Norman decided that this wasn't the life, or death, for him and he would find out if he could work in the cloakroom.

The thought didn't last long, as the ghostly hand of Tabris suddenly flew out of the Portal and gripped Norman tightly by the wrist. Seconds later, he was being forcibly dragged through the Portal with little choice in the matter.

Chapter 9

The Saving of Shaun Mathewson

Eventually, Norman opened his eyes and found himself standing next to Tabris and Morph with the warm early morning sun beating down on his face. Tabris finally released her vice-like grip on his wrist.

Behind them, the Portal swiftly evaporated, as if it were a shallow pool of water thrown into the sands of a desert. In the far distance, the skyscrapers of Los Angeles loomed over the sprawling city like giants guarding their smaller offspring.

Norman loved the feeling of the cool breeze flowing through his hair, the birdsong in the nearby trees and the sparkle in Tabris' eyes as she met his gaze and smiled.

Morph also appeared to enjoy being back on Earth and was sniffing around the grass enquiringly, as if he had recently lost something. In Norman's head, he could hear the word 'chicken' being repeated. After several failed attempts, he finally managed to block Morph's thoughts from his mind.

It dawned on Norman that it was true what Sir Poop had said. He told him that his senses would become more acute—almost superhuman. He felt as if he could hear a bee buzzing at twenty paces or watch an ant crawl on a tree on the other side of the street.

For a split second, Norman considered wearing a cape and red pants on the outside of his trousers, but then dismissed the idea as Tabris approached.

"Shaun must be around here somewhere. You two go over there and I'll scout around in this direction," Tabris said, before moving towards a block of derelict buildings that looked so run down even a stray dog would have thought twice about entering.

Trotting to the brow of the hill in the opposite direction, Morph stared into the distance. Norman followed a few paces behind and realised that they were standing at the top of one of the steepest roads he'd ever seen. In fact, it wasn't just steep, it was unbelievably steep and appeared to run straight down into the pits of the underworld.

At the very bottom of the hill, a large, black, pick-up truck turned and started making its way slowly up the sheer incline; its engine starting to strain against the forces of gravity. As the vehicle approached and the revs grew louder, Tabris moved back towards Norman and squinted in the sunlight.

"I don't like the look of this. If it's what I think it is, Shaun is making life very easy for the Horag."

The truck pulled, heaved and strained itself up the sheer

incline, swung round in a large arc and pulled to a stop facing down the hill several metres from where they were standing.

Inside the cab were three giggling teenagers, who couldn't have been older than eighteen. Norman easily recognised the mess of red hair as their target, Shaun Mathewson.

The boys jumped down from the cab, but left the engine running, presumably to keep the air conditioning on. The driver, a skinny lad wearing basketball shorts, moved to the back of the truck and flipped down the tailgate, revealing a supermarket shopping trolley.

Tabris groaned. "Right, you two need to be on your toes. Remember, you can't move a human, but you can move objects around to keep them safe. Just don't be too obvious. Stay sharp!"

As the trolley was carefully positioned at the top of the hill by the driver and his friend, Shaun removed a pair of swimming goggles from his pocket and placed them delicately over his eyes. His friend had started filming the action on his phone to loud jeers and whoops. Clambering ungainly into the trolley, Shaun sat down and made himself comfortable.

"So, let's run through the plan one more time," the driver said to his friend holding the camera. "I'll give you the faintest of touches with my truck to get you moving, then I'll follow you down the hill measuring the speed all way to the bottom. The record is thirty-eight miles per hour. Got it?"

Shaun gave him a thumbs-up and an enormous grin followed by several rounds of high-fives. The teenagers then climbed back into the cab and fastened their seatbelts securely.

Observing something in the corner of her eye, Tabris spun sharply to face the driver's side of the truck. Emerging from the shadows came a hideous creature, so ugly it would have to sneak up to a mirror.

Large pointed ears protruded past its sloping shoulders. It stood glaring at Tabris with evil, dead eyes. A flat nose, not dissimilar to a pig, sat squished in the middle of its rotund, furry face. Partially hidden within a thin smile that stretched far wider than it should have, was a set of razor-sharp teeth. Even though the monster couldn't have been more than a metre tall, if its ugliness were bricks, it would have been the size of the Great Wall of China.

Like a gunslinger in an old Western, Tabris squared up to the Horag, their eyes locked in combat. To her right stood the pick-up truck with its engine rumbling and to the left, Shaun sat inside his shopping trolley sporting a pair of swimming goggles. Norman and Morph stood in front of the trolley at the brow of the hill.

With amazing agility, the Horag jumped into the cab a second before the driver's door closed and slammed on the truck's gas pedal. Immediately, Tabris leaped up and landed nimbly in the back of the truck, clinging tightly to a roof bar to steady herself.

The vehicle accelerated at incredible speed towards the trolley, situated only a few metres in front. The impact rocked Shaun to the bone as the trolley launched itself towards the edge of the precipice.

Seeing a runaway trolley hurtling towards him at great speed, Morph sprang up into Norman's arms and scrambled up to his shoulders.

A moment later, the metallic cage struck Norman with such force, that his body lifted from the ground and he was left clinging helplessly to the front of the trolley, as it accelerated down the steepest hill in the world.

Completely oblivious to a screaming Norman and Morph, who was now balanced precariously on Norman's head, Shaun recovered his composure and sat upright in the trolley, as it hurtled down the empty road.

The driver was trying to understand how his truck had suddenly lurched forward at remarkable speed. His friend in the passenger seat continued to film exclaiming, "This will be, without doubt, the best movie I will ever upload to YouTube."

The speed on the pickup's dashboard had already reached thirty miles per hour and was increasing steadily. On the back of the truck, Tabris desperately gripped the roof bar and focused her attention on the flimsy shopping trolley now moving at incredible velocity further down the hill.

Dotted all over the road were twigs, empty drink cans and large potholes, any of which could easily de-rail the trolley and send the unprotected Shaun flying to a painful death.

Tabris breathed deeply and concentrated on all the objects in the trolley's path, managing to use her powers to flick items out of the way at the last moment. The deep rutted potholes were a little trickier to manage and she was forced to carefully tilt the trolley left and right to avoid them.

She would have found her work a little easier if she didn't have to contend with the high-pitched screaming coming from Norman, still heroically clinging to the front of the trolley. Perched on top of his shoulder, bristling with fear and with all his claws extended into Norman, squatted a terrified Morph.

"Man, this is awesome! Speed rush or what! He's going fifty-five miles per hour!" exclaimed the driver.

When the trolley had reached halfway down the hill, Tabris noticed that the number of potholes had started to increase, making her task even harder.

Looking through the window, she could now see the speed had increased to sixty-two miles per hour. It was like playing a game of *Super Mario* and guiding him through a minefield at level two thousand.

At that precise moment, a large delivery truck slowly turned into the road, no more than a few hundred yards in front of the speeding trolley. The very solid steel bumper glistened in the sunlight like a guillotine beckoning its next victim.

The delivery driver, looking from left to right for a particular address, seemed oblivious to the scene in front of him, as he purposefully made his way up the hill.

"Norman!" Tabris yelled at the top of her voice. "I'm going to ditch the trolley! Jump!"

For the first time in their lives, both Norman and Morph transmitted the same message at the same time in each other's minds.

"What? No way!"

With only a few metres to spare before the inevitable impact, Tabris threw all her telekinetic energy in the direction of the trolley, which pitched awkwardly to the right.

The metal frame slammed into the kerb with an ear-splitting crash and Norman, followed by Shaun, tumbled head over heels through the long grass outside an empty house next to the road.

When they finally came to a stop on the unkempt lawn, only missing a streetlight by centimetres, they emerged dazed but unhurt. The now unrecognisable trolley lay in a crumpled wreck beside the house.

Unfortunately, Morph had taken a different path. The impact had catapulted him high into the air and for some time he sailed through the cool breeze, only noticing the large pond below him during his rapid descent. He hated water with a passion.

Norman, who had recovered enough to follow the flight path of Morph, watched in astonishment as the water parted in a mini tsunami, sending startled ducks in all directions.

The pick-up truck abruptly came to a stop at the side of the road and Tabris, the driver and his friend, jumped on to the path, keen to see if Shaun still had all his limbs intact. They found him squatting in the grass, rubbing his head and gingerly removing his swimming goggles. The only casualty looked to be his wide grin, which had slipped from his face.

Once Tabris had assured herself that Shaun was safe and the Horag had disappeared, she strolled over to Norman.

"So, you've finally stopped screaming like a six-year-old opera singer then?"

Norman blushed with embarrassment and felt thoroughly ashamed of himself. Tabris punched him on the arm and gave him a forgiving smile.

"Is Morph going to be alright?" Norman asked her tentatively.

"He's already dead. How much worse can he be?"

A look of relief flooded Norman's face and he appeared to relax a little.

An instant later, a shadow appeared just below the surface of the water followed by Morph's soaked head popping out like a submarine's periscope. A piece of pond weed lay draped between his ears.

"Morph, do the doggy paddle! I mean the catty paddle!" Tabris laughed but seeing Morph's expression she unsuccessfully tried to disguise the noise as a cough.

Eventually, Morph staggered on to the bank, dripping wet and looking thoroughly miserable. He directed a piercing glare at Norman, squirted some muddy water from his mouth and, without saying a word, slowly made his way towards a patch of dry grass, collapsed on to his stomach and bathed in the warm sunlight.

By this time, Shaun and his friends were sufficiently recovered to start another round of high-fives in between watching the film that had been recorded. None of them questioned why the truck had suddenly and mysteriously accelerated at the top of the hill.

Shortly afterwards, a chorus of synchronised beeping sounds announced that Tabris, Norman and Morph's time had come to end. Together, they made their way to a grassy patch and Norman could see his Messenger device counting down from sixty seconds.

Tabris pressed the round button on the side of her watch and the Portal re-appeared instantly, shimmering in the sun. This time, Norman had no hesitation following her, whilst a bedraggled Morph slumped along behind.

As if by magic, they all re-emerged into Potts' workshop with the familiar hum of the machinery reverberating in the background.

Potts gave Tabris an enquiring look and she returned the gesture with a smile and thumbs-up.

"Excellent, well done Tabris. I trust your new students were a great help?"

Stepping from the shadows, Norman and Morph moved forward, revealing their dishevelled state.

"Oh dear, maybe not. Well, you two have been in the wars, haven't you?" Potts said sympathetically. "Come on then Morph, let's get you cleaned up. We'll start by taking that pond weed off your head, shall we?"

Chapter 10

The Training

Tabris couldn't hide the concern on her face when Norman and Morph entered the classroom some time later. Her mission as a newly appointed Ghosteleer teacher was to make sure her students passed the exams. If they failed, then Norman and Morph would be outcast into the ether, never to exist again. The enormity of the task weighed heavily on her shoulders, dragging her down like an anchor in the ocean.

Despite the challenge that Norman presented, she knew her determination to never lose a student would be her greatest strength.

Undoubtedly, there were superior teachers at the facility with more experience, but she fiercely believed that no one else would dedicate more time and passion in their duties. Even if she had to spend every waking hour tutoring Norman, that's what she would do.

She cast her eyes over the two pupils sitting attentively at the front desk in the classroom. Norman had cleaned himself up and changed his clothes. Now sporting a fresh red t-shirt and faded jeans, he even looked handsome in his own peculiar way. She had grown particularly fond of Norman since their first encounter. She loved the way he made her laugh and how he never gave up trying to learn, despite not being the most gifted student.

Morph too, had brushed up extremely well after a few hours in Potts' care. His short fur glistened under the bright neon lights in the room. Even his whiskers shimmered like silver threads of silk.

"Okay, we have our work cut out. Maybe I introduced you to the human world a little too early, but now you know what you need to do," Tabris said.

She sat down on a stool situated next to a large white board and explained the subjects they would be learning over the coming weeks. These included how to pass through solid objects in the human world, how to fight Apollyon's Horag soldiers and how to unlock bathroom doors. There's no point waiting outside a toilet when a nasty little Horag can be doing all sorts of things to a human when they are at their most vulnerable.

"Above all, you need to learn how to pace yourselves. When you move objects, it is extremely tiring, and it will exhaust you. If you use up all your energy in the first couple of minutes of a mission, you'll be so weak that you will fail. The bigger the objects you move, the more it will take out of you. Let's talk about moving through walls."

Norman forced himself to sit up straight and instructed his brain to absorb as much information as possible. Occasionally, he would hear Morph's thoughts sweep through his mind like a lost tourist asking for directions. Unsurprisingly, most of the ideas trespassing in his head consisted of poultry related items, such as how he could pass through a solid wall made of chicken. Then he would substitute the word 'pass' with 'eat' and it would lead down a whole new thought avenue.

"You need to adjust your mind into a different state and engage with the molecular structure of the item you want to pass through."

Morph perked up at this point, clarifying with Tabris a quantum mechanics theory that he held, stating if all your particles are primed for tunnelling through a wall, then you can walk through it.

The two of them enthusiastically continued their high-brow conversation about wave functions until Norman accidentally fell off his stool.

"I was just trying to pass through the desk," Norman casually explained, desperately attempting to hide his embarrassment in front of Tabris.

The next learning topic consisted of Horag successes and how Ghosteleers could learn from their mistakes. Over the centuries, Apollyon fighters had killed off many creative humans destined to develop great things in their lifetime.

The first example Tabris recalled involved Monica Meyer, the mayor of Betterton in Maryland, America. She had discovered a combination of chemicals and perfumes that would calm even the angriest of people. One sniff and an irate madman would start handing out flowers to complete strangers.

For some inexplicable reason, in 1980, Mary had decided to check out her town's sewage tanks. She had with her some water testing equipment and a clip attached to a harness that she would secure to a bar on the side of the tank.

Unfortunately for Mary, the Ghosteleer hadn't noticed the Horag a few minutes earlier removing the screws that attached the safety bar to the tank. The ill-fated Mary toppled into the sewage tank and drowned in fifteen feet of human waste. One minute she was high on the sweet smell of success, the next she had sunk in the noxious fumes of something altogether nastier.

Then Tabris recounted the story of Paul G. Thomas, the owner of a wool mill who had plans to revolutionise the Christmas jumper. A callous Horag had greased the floor in front of a vicious-looking spindling machine, resulting in Paul falling head first into the inner workings of the mechanism. When the police finally arrived, the doomed Mr Thomas lay wrapped within a giant ball of wool that rolled gently across the room.

After several more gruesome examples, Tabris decided that they could break for the day, much to the relief of Norman and his throbbing forehead.

For homework, they were assigned a session in the bowling alley, located at the far end of the facility. Throwing some balls towards a few skittles sounded infinitely better than three hours of algebra, which had been the last homework Norman had received in his school days.

*

The heavy-set door to the bowling alley swung open easily, revealing a bright and spacious room with several occupied lanes. *Wrecking Ball* by Miley Cyrus played noisily in the background.

At the far end of the room, Nick and Lynn were standing over a collection of colourful balls having an animated discussion.

"Lynn, you're a cheat and you know it," Nick exclaimed in a steady voice straining with frustration.

"You're just a bad loser, that's all," retorted Lynn, smiling smugly.

"Well, let's get Norman and Morph's opinion then," said Nick. "Morph, you're with me and Norman, you can go with Lynn. The rules of the game are the same as normal bowling, except you aren't allowed to touch the ball after you place it on the floor. Using only your telekinetic powers, you must push the ball down the lane and knock over as many pins as possible. Once the ball has passed the second line marked in red, a few metres down the lane, you must not interfere with the ball again."

Nick glared accusingly at Lynn as he strongly emphasised the last sentence. Ignoring Nick, Lynn reset the scores and picked up a glossy red ball, sprinkled liberally with glitter so that it sparkled in the bright overhead lights. She walked assuredly to the starting line and gently placed the ball down on to the lightly coloured floor.

Slowly, she took two steps back and crouched down, lining up the ball with the skittles. As she raised both of her hands, the ball started moving all by itself, rapidly gaining speed as it flew down the lane. She stood upright as the ball sailed past the red line and headed towards the wooden targets in the distance.

All but two pins flew everywhere with a satisfying crash. Lynn scowled at the remaining stubborn pegs and picked up another ball from the rack. The next ball travelled down the lane in precisely the same way and cleanly picked off the two lingering pins.

Lynn turned with a satisfied look upon her face and invited Morph to have a go. Nick helped to select a ball and positioned it behind the line. Morph strolled up to the ball and started circling it like a predator stalking its prey. Eventually, he sat behind it and looked down the lane to the ten pins located at the end.

Norman watched as Morph's whiskers twitched and the ball started accelerating at fantastic speed. As it approached the pins it drifted further and further out towards the gutter, finally just missing the outside skittle.

"Good effort, Morph," Nick said encouragingly and placed another ball in the starting position.

For his second attempt, Morph followed his same routine and hurtled the ball down the lane, only this time it appeared to be going even faster. It smashed into the side of the front pin with such force that all the other players in the alley stopped what they were doing and stood watching in amazement. Every pin had not only fallen; some had shattered into shards of wood, with splinters hurtling in all directions.

"Bravo, Morph!" exclaimed Nick, clapping his hands enthusiastically. "Although you may want to tone it down a bit or we'll run out of pins."

After a brief clean up and pin replacement, Norman stepped up to the starting line and placed the heaviest ball he could find softly on the floor. He thought that if he could get the ball moving, its weight would send the pins flying or at least topple them.

He crouched down behind the ball, placing his palms on his thighs and began eyeing up the distance to the pins. Just then, the memory of his first effort at moving objects flew into his mind and he realised that whilst he was in this crouching position, there was a very high risk of more wind escaping. Panicking, he quickly stood upright pulling the ball rapidly through his open legs and over the toes of Lynn who was sitting directly behind him.

An ear-splitting expletive echoed around the alley and for the second time that evening, all the players stopped and looked over to the end lane.

Chapter 11

The Written Exam

An exciting rumour had been spreading like wildfire throughout the facility. The speculation alleged there would soon be a visit from the most revered President, Ms Thorne. Her visits were rare and when they did occur, it usually preceded a special announcement or grand occasion.

Ms Thorne had achieved almost legendary status within the organisation and still held the record for saving more humans during her time as a Ghosteleer than anyone else (Silas included). She was also the most feared person in the facility by a long margin.

The gossip reached Tabris during one of her extra training sessions with Norman. For weeks, they had studied almost every night, covering subjects such as 'beanbag juggling' and 'hunt the Horag,' in which Tabris dressed up in a furry onesie.

Most exercises resulted in large amounts of giggling, which although fun, didn't do much to progress Norman's abilities.

Morph spent many of his evenings with Potts discussing the merits of nuclear fusion and whether the residents of Earth would use the unlimited power on heating toilet seats. The pair now enjoyed a truly close, trusted bond.

Morph also kept a close eye on Silas, who would occasionally drop into the shadows to partake in mysterious, whispered conversations with fellow Ghosteleers. There was something about the man that made Morph's coat bristle.

It was late in the week when Sir Poop interrupted Norman and Morph's joint lesson. They were studying the case of Jimi Allamby, the owner of an electric two-wheeled scooter. In 2010, he had driven the device off the edge of a cliff, but only after a Horag had placed a diversion sign in the middle of the road with an arrow that pointed in the wrong direction.

Inviting Tabris to the far corner of the room, Sir Poop spoke very quietly so that only the two of them could hear what he said. "The President will be arriving any day now and we need to complete the training. How soon will it be before Norman is ready to take the exam?"

Deep down Tabris knew this day would eventually come but hoped it wouldn't be so soon.

"I think July would be fine," she said hesitantly.

"But that's two months away!" exclaimed Sir Poop a little louder than he should have.

"I didn't mean this July! I was thinking maybe next year."

Sir Poop slumped on a nearby desk and exhaled a long, deep breath. Summoning all his strength, he addressed Norman and Morph, who looked over at his dishevelled state with keen interest.

"Afternoon gentlemen. Unfortunately, time is against us and we must move your exam date forward. The President has declared that all training must be completed immediately. The exam will have to take place tomorrow morning."

"What?" cried Norman and Tabris in unison. Morph looked quite happy to get the test over with.

"I know it is faster than we all would have liked, but it can't be helped. There will be a written test in the morning followed by a practical test in the afternoon. If you pass both exams, then you will be fully fledged Ghosteleers. But remember, because of your special connection, the pair of you have to pass."

Feeling the angry stare from Tabris penetrating his back like daggers, Sir Poop decided this would be a good time to leave.

"I wish you the very best of luck. See you tomorrow," Sir Poop said before he left the room, moving very swiftly for such a large man.

*

If Norman could have slept, he would have slept badly. Failing this exam meant that both him and Morph would be banished to the 'other side,' never to exist again. This was pressure on an unprecedented scale and the evening moved by slower than a geriatric slug.

The next day, Sir Poop stood patiently waiting at the front of the class as Norman and Morph cautiously entered. Tabris sat sullenly on a stool, convinced that

Norman could never succeed. Any casual observer in the room would find it extremely difficult to judge who looked the most nervous.

Norman and Morph sat down on the two allocated seats that were positioned either side of the room. In front of them lay a two-sided sheet of white paper, printed with fifty multiple choice questions. They had to get at least forty correct to pass.

"Gentlemen, you may look up for inspiration, down in desperation, but not left and right for information. You may begin," Sir Poop said.

A large clock mounted on the front desk started counting down from sixty minutes. Morph used his telekinetic powers to pick up a pencil and immediately started to tick off the boxes.

Norman felt his palms sweat and stared at the first question, which he read over and over and over again. The more he stared at the words, the more they seem to transform into ant-like letters and scuttle around the page.

1. *Which of the following objects must you not directly move in the human world?*

    a. A cup of tea, because it may be hot

    b. A toilet brush, because the germs may kill you

    c. A human, because that is against the Ghosteleer law

    d. A hedgehog, because although they look cute, their spines are deadly

It was as if every brain cell in Norman's head decided this would be a good time to go on holiday. *Maybe somewhere hot with a nice beach and ice cream?* He found himself having to repeatedly shake his head to stop drifting off into another daydream.

The clock ticked by at what felt like double speed and eventually Sir Poop gave a five-minute warning.

Morph had finished the test around thirty minutes earlier and nervously looked up at Norman, knowing that his fate was precariously held in his hands. Norman had already killed him once and he didn't feel like letting him do it again.

Norman heard the clear, crisp tones of Morph float inside his mind. *'What number are you on?'*

"Nine," came Norman's frustrated reply.

"You're joking? Argh! Okay, write this down. Nine a, ten c, eleven b. . ."

Using his mind powers to communicate with Norman, Morph then proceeded to provide all the answers to the questions as the blissfully ignorant Sir Poop looked on.

Norman laid the pencil down the very moment the clock reached zero and started soothing his aching hand.

In a swift movement, Sir Poop collected the papers and returned to the front of the classroom, leaving the two anxious students sitting quietly at opposite ends of the room.

The scratching sound of pencil on paper noisily echoed around the room as the marking took place. Finally, Sir Poop stood after what felt like an eternity, to the two expectant pupils and anxious teacher.

"Morph, congratulations. You have scored forty-nine out

of fifty. You failed the very last question asking what the most important part of being a Ghosteleer is. You answered, 'Finding and eating chicken,' when of course the answer is, 'Finding and saving humans.'

"My answer sounds fine to me," murmured Morph under his breath.

Sir Poop then turned to face Norman who instantly felt the piercing, suspicious eyes bore into him. "Norman, congratulations to you too. You got the first eight questions wrong, but then you managed to get every question right except for the last one. You also stated that you believe finding and saving a chicken is the most important part of being a Ghosteleer. Still, you achieved forty-one out of fifty and have passed the written test."

Tabris squeaked in delight and started clapping her hands enthusiastically. Norman let out a sigh of relief.

"Thanks Morph," Norman said telepathically, as Morph wiped his furry brow with his paw.

Chapter 12

The Deputy

The successful completion of the written exam meant that Norman and Morph were halfway to being fully qualified Ghosteleers. They just needed to pass the practical test.

Norman's emotions consisted of a heady mix of euphoria—having passed the test—versus apprehension for what would be about to come. Morph on the other hand, displayed a combination of cool confidence and shiny whiskers.

Sir Poop handed a folder to Tabris containing the details of the human they must save. The spiritual lives of Norman and Morph depended on it. She had just one hour to prepare her students before they would pass through the Portal into the uncertain world that awaited them.

Their target was the deputy mayor of Delhi, Surinder Singh Bajwa. He lived on the eighth floor, in one of the city's high-rise apartments and had spent years building strong relationships with food manufacturers around the world. It would be through these connections that he would, in time, invent a tasty, chicken-flavoured treat for cats everywhere. If Morph needed any more motivation to save a human, it couldn't get any better than this!

Tabris studiously took Norman and Morph through all the possible options on where the Horag could be hiding, potential hazards and areas to stay clear of. Under no circumstances should they let Surinder out on to the balcony, as a fall from eight floors up wouldn't be good for his health, or their chances of becoming fully qualified Ghosteleers.

As the final minutes counted down, the group headed towards Potts' Portal Room where Morph casually strolled through his purpose-built cat-flap. Tabris and Norman entered the room a short while later, followed by Sir Poop who had rushed to catch them up. A bead of sweat trickled down the forehead of Sir Poop as he described the rules of the final test.

On the other side of the room, Potts was busily preparing the necessary equipment. In addition to the Messenger device and cat collar, Potts also placed a small drone on the master console. The flying gadget looked like a jammy dodger, but it was powerful enough to transmit video and sound back to the large screens hanging randomly around Potts' laboratory. The images would determine whether Norman and Morph had passed their final assessment.

When Morph's collar had been securely fastened by

Potts, Sir Poop addressed them for the final time prior to their departure.

"You will have the usual sixty minutes to find your target and keep him alive until the Messenger alarm sounds. Once you are through the Portal, the drone will take off automatically and track your every move. It is designed to be almost invisible, so do not concern yourself when it flies off."

The humming of the machinery in the room seemed to amplify as he finished giving his instructions. The Portal shimmered its usual blue glow and appeared to silently beckon Norman and his feline companion to their destiny, whatever that might be.

"Go save him, boys," Sir Poop said, patting Norman on the back.

Tabris remained silent. She had a look of nervous fear in her eyes but forced an encouraging smile to play on her face.

Norman looked down at Morph who returned his gaze with a steely determination and together they strode purposefully towards the Portal. Norman stepped through first, feeling the familiar tingling sensation as the sparkling light spread through his body.

Seconds later, both he and Morph were standing in a quiet, pot-holed dirt track squashed between two high-rise buildings. Even though they were swallowed by deep, dark shadows, the stifling heat attacked them like flaming daggers.

At the end of the alleyway, a busy, bustling street greeted them. A cacophony of sounds, smells and sights bombarded their already overwhelmed senses and for a minute they both stood open-mouthed, desperately trying to absorb the chaotic scene.

The tiny drone sprang into life, emitting a high-pitched buzz, as the four small rotor blades spun furiously. It swiftly lifted from Norman's outstretched hand and gracefully disappeared behind a computer repair shop on the other side of the street.

Cautiously, Morph attempted to cross the road, taking care to avoid the dogs, cows, bikes, trucks and cars, which were stationary due to the snarled-up traffic.

"I think Surinder's apartment is over there," shouted Morph above the noise of the constant hooting of car horns. He nodded towards a light orange-coloured building behind a small forest of palm trees.

Norman obediently followed Morph down the street being careful not to bump into anyone or anything that was coming in the opposite direction.

Even though nobody alive could see or hear the trainee Ghosteleers, it would simply be rude to walk right through a little old lady out for her daily shop. More than once, Norman had to stop himself from an unpleasant stroll right into the backside of a cow.

The pair eventually arrived at the prestigious Goldleaf Apartments without any major concerns, other than the fact it had taken them fifteen minutes to navigate one hundred metres through a seriously congested street.

The building consisted of a mishmash of different shapes jumbled together as if the architect had thrown a handful of Lego in the air and where they landed was the final design.

There were two main walls facing each other, both with a vertical line of balconies stretching up to the tenth floor. Every platform had a dark awning to protect the inhabitants from the glaring midday sun, but most had been collapsed down to allow the gentler evening light to filter through the large patio windows.

The address Norman and Morph had been given by Tabris was 804b Goldleaf Apartments. Facing them in the main courtyard were two unmarked doors that headed to different parts of the building. Only one entrance would take them to Surinder. If they chose the wrong doorway, valuable time and potentially a life, would be lost.

Norman decided that playing rock, paper, scissors would be the fairest way to select which one of them would choose the entrance. On the count of three, Norman opted for scissors; and lost. It hadn't occurred to him that Morph could only do rock with his paws.

Morph chose the path that veered to the right and approached a stainless-steel lift, opposite an empty reception area. Using his telekinetic powers, Morph pressed the up arrow for the lift. The doors instantly slid open allowing them to step inside the mirrored enclosure. Norman selected floor eight and the doors gently began to close.

"Norman, stop thinking about passing through solid objects! Now is not the time!" cried Morph.

"Tabris told me to take every opportunity in the human world to practise," replied Norman stubbornly. "Why shouldn't I?"

The lift started its ascent, at which point the floor began

to move up Norman's foot, past his ankles and towards his knees. Norman looked down, surprised to see Morph and the floor heading steadily upwards whilst he stood still. He felt as though he were sinking in quicksand, about to be swallowed by a sticky, brown coloured carpet.

"Oh, I see your point now."

As Morph continued to rise, he gave Norman a cold, stony glare that was particularly piercing when their eyes were level.

Norman looked suitably guilty as their heads passed only centimetres apart. Seconds later, Norman found himself alone in an empty lift shaft.

Slowly he made his way into the reception area and noticed a sign for the stairs in the far corner. Heaving a big sigh, Norman reluctantly started the long trudge to the eighth floor. He already felt exhausted and drained by the intense heat as well as the journey from the Portal.

When the lift doors finally opened, the warm glow of the evening sun flooded the small compartment. Morph trotted out and took in his surroundings.

A long corridor on the outside of the building stretched into the distance. There were solid, expensive-looking doors spaciously spread out left and right. Next to each entrance were apartment numbers, followed with the letter A.

Morph's heart sank as he realised he had entered the wrong complex. He jumped carefully up onto the handrail and stared at the apartments located in the opposite building. All their numbers ended with the letter B.

A loud banging noise suddenly echoed through the hot

air, followed by wild screeching. A fuming, plump man stood on the balcony on the opposite tower whilst a pack of half a dozen large monkeys tore at his clothes. Behind the monkeys, a Horag beamed gleefully, dancing excitedly from one foot to the other.

Morph looked on in horror. He'd never felt this helpless. *"Norman! Get to the courtyard at the side of the building! Quick!"*

A breathless Norman heard the voice inside his head as clearly as if Morph were standing beside him. He glanced up at the number six on the stairwell, sighed and headed back the way he'd come. At least he would have gravity on his side for the downward journey.

Surinder picked up a broom handle and valiantly fought the attacking monkeys that had congregated on his plush balcony. The path back to his lounge had been completely cut off by snarling teeth and sharp, pointed claws.

The group gradually pushed Surinder closer to the edge of the balcony as the stranded Morph looked on.

The Horag glanced across at Morph and smiled a cold and evil grin. There would be no tasty chicken snacks in this world.

Surinder was now pressed firmly against the edge of the balcony. Below him was a fearful drop of eight floors and a concrete patio.

The Horag continued to poke a stick at the enraged primates, taunting them further. Their rage had now reached fever pitch and they rushed at Surinder, eventually forcing him over the edge of the rail.

Morph looked on in dismay as the grappling figure

shrieked and toppled over the railing, swiftly heading for the ground below.

Quick as a flash, Morph used his powers to extend an awning attached to the apartment below. The dark coloured material stretched tightly and Surinder bounced off the canopy and flew through the air towards the next awning.

Morph performed the same trick several times over as the falling figure rebounded like a marble in a pinball machine.

After bouncing off awnings for five floors, Morph's powers finally stopped working. The distance between him and Norman had grown too great for his telekinetic powers.

Outside, Norman staggered into the courtyard, panting breathlessly from his race down the stairs. He looked up at the screaming Surinder, who appeared to be zig-zagging his way down, bouncing off various awnings as he fell.

Suddenly, no more canopies opened, and the deputy mayor hurtled downwards to the solid floor at tremendous speed.

Norman spun around in panic looking for something that could help the situation. He saw a watering can, a rake, an ornamental cat and a football. There simply wasn't anything useful! Then, he spotted it. A laundry cart, half-filled with dirty bed sheets, had just been wheeled around the corner by a cleaning lady wearing headphones.

Norman closed his eyes, stretched out his hands, pointed his fingers and pushed the trolley with his mind. A feeling of enormous power surged through his body and out of his pointed fingers.

The laundry cart lurched forward just as Surinder dropped heavily with a loud thump into a tangle of cotton sheets.

For a moment, complete stillness descended upon the courtyard. High above, the Horag's smile slipped from his ugly face.

Slowly, the contents of the cart began to stir, and a golden pillowcase emerged from the mess of laundry like a beautiful sunrise. A pair of hands lifted the material up, revealing a trembling and mightily relieved Surinder.

Racing down the stairs and onto the patio, Morph pulled up in front of Norman and opened his mouth, except no sound came out. He tried a few more times and eventually managed to stutter, "Norman. You did it! You saved Surinder. And you saved us!"

Norman still had his eyes tightly shut. Gradually, he forced one eyelid open and stared at the scene in front of him, not daring to believe the deputy major had survived. Several minutes went by before Morph could persuade Norman to lower his hands and open his other eye.

Several metres away, Surinder had clambered over the side of the laundry cart and was enthusiastically hugging the legs of the nearby cleaning woman, convinced that she had pushed the trolley into his path.

She had no idea who this mad person kneeling in front of her was, but there was a good chance she might get a tip, so she willingly accepted the praise.

The sound of an alarm rang through the warm air, startling Norman, who looked around in fright. The Messenger device had started beeping. Norman took a second to compose himself and gratefully pressed the button to reactivate the Portal.

As he did so, the high-pitched whining of the mini drone became louder. He held out his hand and it landed gently in his palm before the white and red rota blades stopped spinning.

Together, Morph and Norman triumphantly strode through the Portal and back into Potts' laboratory.

Chapter 13

The Celebrations

As Norman stepped through the Portal into the laboratory, a flying object almost knocked him clean off his feet. His nerves, which were already in shreds, felt on the brink of packing up and heading off for a very long holiday.

Only after a few seconds did he realise Tabris had her arms wrapped tightly around him in an enormous bear hug. This was, without question, the best day of his life—and death—combined. Even Morph purred loudly, as Potts tickled him under his chin.

"Excellent work!" Sir Poop beamed, clapping his hands enthusiastically. "You left it a bit late, but Surinder survived and that is the most crucial thing. You have passed the entrance exams and I can happily confirm you are both now fully qualified Ghosteleers. Congratulations!"

The video screens around the room displayed a still

image of the deputy major, still on his knees, embracing the cleaning woman. Norman looked up at the picture and a wave of pride swelled through his body. This achievement felt even better than the time he swam the width of the local swimming pool in his pyjamas.

Norman and Morph embraced the celebrations, cheers and compliments. Everyone had their favourite moment in the adventure, which they happily narrated in great detail.

Nick and Lynn then entered the room, keen to discover the fate of Norman and Morph. This gave the collection a new reason to recount the stories with even more embellishment.

When the festivities finally calmed, Norman and Morph departed for a relaxing afternoon in the Garden Room with Nick and Lynn.

"At tonight's ceremony, there's a rumour that Ms Thorne will be making an announcement," Lynn exclaimed eagerly.

The ceremony was the respected Passing Away ritual, when Ghosteleers who had put in more than five years' duty had the option of 'resting in peace in a place of eternal beauty.' Well that's how Sir Poop liked to promote it.

"What type of announcement?" enquired Morph.

"I heard someone say that the Rescuer has appeared on Earth."

"Rubbish. That's nothing more than a Ghosteleer legend created by desperate leaders trying to motivate their staff," said Nick, rolling his eyes in disbelief.

"It's true!" Lynn cried. "The Rescuer can bring everyone on the planet together! Can you imagine a world with no more fighting? People working together to create peace and provide food for the hungry?"

"If that person exists," mused Morph. "They would certainly be the number one target for Apollyon and his Horag soldiers. Good luck to the Ghosteleer fighting that particular battle."

Norman shuddered at the thought and stretched out next to Morph on the trimmed, green grass.

*

The Passing Away ceremony took place later that evening in the large, majestic conference room. Tasteful decorations were dotted on the round tables spread randomly throughout the chamber and stunning frescos adorned the light-coloured ceiling. Enormous chandeliers hung like stalactites, throwing soft light into the regal setting, whilst a plush, thick pile carpet swallowed up any foot that dared tread on it. At the front of the room, a polished wooden stage imposed itself over the scene.

When the entrance doors finally swung open, a flood of people spilled in, transforming the tranquillity of the chamber into a noisy, bustling metropolis. Everyone in the academy had been invited and all of them were dressed in their finest outfits.

Norman and Morph stood gazing in wonder at the paintings adorned on every wall.

"Impressive, aren't they?" said Tabris following their stare. "None other than the work of Leonardo Da Vinci himself."

"Seriously?" questioned Morph.

"Absolutely. It was before my time here, but Sir Poop often recalls his experiences with him. Apparently, he made an awful Ghosteleer. He kept insisting on taking his catapult with him to fight the Horags. By the time he set it up, the human would be long gone. In the end, he was asked to do painting and decorating instead. His drawings were good, but he was rubbish at wallpapering."

Morph sat on a cushioned seat next to Potts, who had spent several happy hours brushing his fur and perfecting his whiskers. Also seated at their table were Norman, Lynn, Nick and Tabris. Nobody could sit still as the excitement crackled through the air.

A spotlight sprang into life and illuminated the podium at the centre of the stage. A hush descended upon the room.

Sir Poop emerged from the left-hand side of the stage and confidently made his way towards the podium.

A warm round of applause echoed around the room. A small cheer of, "Poop, Poop, Poop," could be heard from a table in the far corner.

Sir Poop held up his hand in acknowledgement of the welcome and the clapping gradually subsided.

"Fellow Ghosteleers," he announced enthusiastically into the microphone. His voice boomed around the chamber. "Welcome to the Passing Away ceremony."

A loud cheer erupted around the room followed by more applause.

"Tonight, we not only celebrate the Passing Away of Trevor but we also welcome two new Ghosteleers into our family."

Norman could feel his face going bright red as every pair of eyes in the room turned to look at him.

"I'd also like to welcome a very special guest to the stage. She is without doubt the greatest Ghosteleer in history. Ladies and gentlemen, I am honoured to present the President of the Ghosteleer Society, Ms Thorne."

A huge roar erupted, deafening Morph so much that he put his paws over his ears. Everyone stood, clapping hard, as the curtain twitched and out stepped Ms Thorne on to the stage.

Even over the thunderous applause, her footsteps could still be heard hammering down on the stage like nails in a coffin. Her stone face showed no emotion as she made her way purposefully to one of the seats next to the podium.

As she sat facing the audience, her chiselled, angular features became more prominent under the glare of the spotlight. Her eyes, cold as they were, held an obvious intellect that was second to none. Formidable indeed.

Sir Poop settled the crowd and returned to the matters in hand. "Trevor? Would you like to come up on stage please?"

A man in his late fifties, with a huge grin, stood at a table near the front of the room and started to make his way eagerly towards the stage. He bounded up the steps and greeted Sir Poop with an enthusiastic handshake.

"Trevor, it is with great pride and privilege that we send you on to your next afterlife destination. During your five years' service as a Ghosteleer, you have saved a total of one hundred and eight lives and performed your duty impeccably."

Cheers rang around the room until Trevor became a little emotional and wiped away a tear.

"So, without further ado," continued Sir Poop. "I'd like to ask Ms Thorne to conclude the Passing Away."

Sir Poop reached to the top of the podium and carefully lifted a golden, jewel-encrusted dagger. Light bounced in all directions as the handle appeared to dance under the spotlights. Morph could hear gasps from the people at nearby tables.

Very gently, Sir Poop offered the handle of the dagger to Ms Thorne, who gripped it tightly in her bony hand. She then turned to face Trevor.

"See you on the other side!" shouted Trevor, waving enthusiastically to his friends in the audience.

Ms Thorne cut away Trevor's Messenger, which fell uselessly to the floor, and pointed the outstretched blade ominously in his direction.

Trevor reached forward, gently pressed his finger against the point of the dagger and immediately started to dissolve. First his legs disappeared, then his torso, until the only remaining part of him was his smile. Then, that too, vanished into thin air.

Sir Poop took to the podium once more. "Now, please welcome to the stage our new Ghosteleers, Norman and Morph!"

Polite applause sprinkled throughout the room, as Morph jumped down from the table and led the way to the stage. Norman concentrated hard on not tripping, especially when he reached the steps leading to the platform.

They stood facing Sir Poop who picked up two Messenger devices from the top of the podium; one being a specially designed cat collar.

Ms Thorne stood impassively to the side of Sir Poop while he fastened the devices to the newly qualified Ghosteleers.

When Sir Poop finished the presentation to Norman and Morph, the audience dutifully applauded once more. Morph noticed that the only person not clapping was Silas, who had a look of disgust plastered across his face. He believed letting an idiot and a cat into the Ghosteleer family lowered its values.

Morph and Norman returned to their seats, as Ms Thorne, wearing an immaculate black business suit, approached the podium gracefully. Her dignified presence dominated the room, and many sat open-mouthed, awe-struck by her silent power.

She paused at the podium and gazed around the room, as if assessing everyone within it. Nobody dared utter a sound.

"I'm very pleased to see that the saving of humans has increased by three point four percent over the last year. You are all doing a good job and I hope it continues." The complimentary words spoken by Ms Thorne jarred with her menacing appearance. It was like a scorpion pretending to be a kitten. "Without your dedication, humans would surely destroy themselves, leading to the end of the world and victory for Apollyon and his gang of horrid Horags."

The Head of the Ghosteleers paused for dramatic effect, aware of the bombshell she was about to drop. Everyone in the room held their breath.

Philip Beicken

"Some of you may know the legend of the Rescuer. The super human who can unite all the people in the world. Someone who can bring peace to conflict, light to darkness and above all hope where there is fear. Tonight, I can tell you, that person exists!"

Sharp intakes of breath sounded throughout the room, as wide-eyed Ghosteleers stared in disbelief towards the stage. Ms Thorne let the surprised murmurs sweep through the room before raising her hand. Instantly, the room fell silent.

"We don't know very much at this stage other than the fact that this person is in Europe. I have no doubt that Apollyon is also aware of this person's existence and that he is plotting their downfall at this very moment. I cannot emphasise strongly enough that if the Rescuer dies, the fate of the human world looks very grim indeed."

Most of the audience looked pale, stunned and unable to comprehend the significance of the speech. The destiny of the human world rested on a single person and they were up against the full might of Apollyon's army.

"The task of saving this very special human is great indeed. It will require cunning, strength, courage and skill. I can think of no one better to perform this vital mission than Silas," Ms Thorne said.

A great cheer rang out from around the room. Many of the Ghosteleers started chanting, "Silas! Silas! Silas!"

"I have nothing further to add at this time other than I expect the battle to take place sometime during the next month. Whilst I gather more information, I'll be personally

84

supervising the specialist training required for Silas. Thank you for your attention."

Ms Thorne turned and left the stage, leaving Sir Poop to conclude the proceedings.

The excited, but slightly scared crowd, stood and withdrew from the room in a great flurry. Everyone spoke animatedly about who the Rescuer could be, where the battle would take place and which Horag would be sent to do the job. Throughout the entire academy, everyone agreed that Silas would be the best chance the humans would have. Everyone except Morph that is.

Chapter 14

The Discovery

An incredible buzz electrified the atmosphere within the academy. Not a single conversation took place without some sort of speculation on the future of the planet or glowing admiration for the great Silas.

For the last few days he had been away with Ms Thorne at a secret training facility. Morph appeared to be the only Ghosteleer grateful for his absence, since he would tread on his tail at every opportunity. The friction between the two had intensified recently, particularly when Potts had innocently suggested to Silas that Morph could provide some competition on the leader board.

Morph had settled into his Ghosteleer role a little quicker than Norman. The pair had completed two missions since the Passing Away ceremony, both of which were successful. Now, they had a third assignment involving an American entrepreneur, Miss Adams.

The Ghosteleers transported through the Portal as usual and emerged into the hazy glare of the early evening sun. Gargantuan cliffs rose from the dusty ground, reaching up to the cotton wool clouds high above.

The Grand Canyon was indeed a place of awe-inspiring beauty, which is why Anabelle Adams had chosen to spend a few days of her vacation hiking through it. She prided herself on being a long-legged, experienced walker who carried every essential item she could find, including a sun umbrella that doubled as a walking stick. It was this self-made invention that would eventually make her fortune—if she survived the day.

"Morph, I've been thinking," blurted Norman.

His feline companion almost tripped over his tail in surprise. This was a first as far as Morph was concerned!

"I need to do this mission by myself," Norman continued earnestly. "I can't keep existing in your shadow. I have to be able to save someone on my own. This will be an easy one. There's nobody about, the river's really shallow and there is nothing around for miles."

Morph felt that Norman's keenness to impress Tabris had much more to do with him completing the mission than anything else.

"Okay, Norman. This one is yours."

They tailed Anabelle for ten minutes as she followed the meandering river, gently cutting its way through the golden canyon. Californian condors floated graciously in the clear skies above. Somewhere in the distance, the deep rumble of a car engine bounced off the towering cliff face.

Norman instantly flexed his Ghosteleer senses, tuning his eyes to the smallest movement. High above the cliff face, well out of sight, a Horag had taken the opportunity—while a car pulled away—to drop a stone, roughly the size of a tennis ball, off the edge of the cliff. During its rapid descent, it struck a basketball-sized boulder, which also started to move very rapidly towards an even larger piece of rock below.

Norman and Morph observed the rock fall high above Anabelle and each of them quickly formed a counter plan. If just two of the strong trees growing next to the cliff face bent ever so slightly over, they would deflect the falling stones safely away from Anabelle. Simple and effective.

"Ready Norman?"

"Oh, yes, easy," replied a confident Norman.

"Three, two, one, now!"

Morph looked at the trees. But they didn't move. Not even a branch twitched. Instead, Anabelle's umbrella surprisingly opened above her head.

A curious look appeared on Miss Adams' face shortly before she disappeared under the weight of a small mountain. A thunderous boom rolled through the valley like a freight train as the rocks struck the floor, followed by a cloud of dust that rose high into the crisp air. Finally, a stillness shrouded the scene that would have been appropriate in an undertaker's shop. Miss Adams' time on Earth had come to a flat end.

"I can't help but notice that your plan differed slightly

from mine," said Morph. "Do you think it best, perhaps, that we work as a team in future?"

"Err, yes. That might be a good idea," conceded Norman glumly.

*

After returning to the academy, Morph excused himself—he had a hypothesis to mull over. Norman felt particularly deflated and decided to contemplate the failed mission in the stillness of the Garden Room.

Even the tranquillity of the large open space and the trickling stream did little to calm his stresses. He concluded that reflection is fine, as long as you know what to do differently next time. Otherwise, it's self-torture.

"Norman? Morph said you might be here."

Tabris stepped hesitantly across the long, soft grass to where Norman was sitting and knelt beside him.

"Potts told me what happened. You can't save everyone you know. They've all got to go sometime. I've lost hundreds of people and I'm a teacher."

"Yes, but you've also saved thousands. I'm not sure I'll be able to get into double figures," responded Norman miserably.

"I bet there are loads of things you can do well if you had a little more confidence."

With that Tabris lent in to kiss Norman.

Suddenly, the gloom that fogged Norman's head lifted as he realised his day was about to get a great deal better. He shut his eyes and prepared himself for a smooch that he had only ever considered in his wildest imagination.

"NORMAN!" screamed Morph's unexpected voice inside his head.

The startling shout jolted Norman from his special moment with such force he unwittingly head-butted Tabris, who collapsed back on to the grass holding her forehead in pain.

"Not now Morph!" pleaded Norman telepathically in return.

"It can't wait! Meet me now in Potts' lab. It's life or death."

Norman climbed to his feet. "I'm so sorry Tabris. I need to get Morph."

He may have blown his friendship and any potential relationship with Tabris, but Morph was family and he still felt responsible for killing him in the first place.

"Norman, it's fine. Go if you need to," replied a dazed Tabris, still clutching her head.

The sprint to Potts' lab took less than four minutes, plus another couple to get through the security system. Norman finally arrived, out of breath and bent over, trying to get some air back in his lungs. When he finally looked up, he noticed that Potts' face had drained of all colour.

Morph was pacing in front of the Portal console like a tightly sprung tiger in a cage.

"We have to go back through the Portal," exclaimed Morph seriously.

"What? We've only just returned! Besides, my Messenger device isn't flashing. What's going on?"

"I can't really explain, but it's our job to save the Rescuer."

"The Rescuer? No, it isn't. It's Silas' job."

Norman looked to Potts for confirmation, but the stricken man stood impassively with a look of doubt in his eyes.

"Please, both of you," implored Morph. "I can feel that something just isn't right and if we don't act fast, terrible things will happen. I know this makes no sense, but I'm asking you to trust me. The Rescuer is in great peril and time is very much against us. Norman, I've never asked you for anything, except chicken maybe, but please do this for me. And Potts, I know you are taking a huge risk in letting us go through the Portal, but I promise I won't let you down."

Both men stared long and hard at Morph, who undoubtedly had the best instincts in the facility. This could easily mean banishment, or worse, if they were caught. Eventually, after a long pause, they both nodded their heads in agreement.

Having made his decision, Potts started flying around the lab flicking switches, pressing buttons and preparing the camera drone they had used during their exam.

"Take the drone with you just so I can see how you're getting on," said Potts. "There is a slight problem though. I still don't know who the Rescuer is or what they look like. The data hasn't come through yet. I only know the destination."

"We can't wait. We'll just have to guess who the target is."

"It could be anyone!" cried Norman in an alarmed high-pitched voice.

"We can do it," replied Morph trying to sound more confident than he actually felt. In reality, he knew their chance of success was slimmer than a dieting super model that had been run over by a steam roller. They literally had a ghost of a chance.

With the final preparations complete, the Ghosteleers, carrying the drone, hurried through the Portal to an unfamiliar location, to save a human they didn't know, from a terror they couldn't imagine.

*

They found themselves in a deserted, grey, cobbled street in the dead of night. A bright full moon hung high in the heavens, illuminating the old buildings with an eerie glow. Wispy clouds swept across the sky whilst long, dark shadows appeared to swallow every sound.

Just ahead, a silvery glow flooded through an opening between two ancient houses. Norman and Morph cautiously headed towards the gap. Both Ghosteleers could feel the hairs on the back of their necks tingling.

The mini camera drone suddenly sprang to life, making Norman jump clean off the ground. The high-pitched whine of its tiny blades died away, as it rapidly flew above a nearby roof and disappeared from view.

The pair slowly peered around the edge of the wall.

Stretching high into the sky at an impossible angle stood the Leaning Tower of Pisa. The circular building appeared like a ghostly wedding cake, with tier upon tier of archways supported by thin columns of pale stone. Darkness swamped the top of each archway where the bright moon was unable to penetrate.

"Okay, so we're in Italy," said Morph, as if that helped the situation.

"But where is the Rescuer? This place is deserted and it's giving me the creeps. It feels as if it's haunted."

Morph shook his head in disbelief at Norman and twitched his whiskers. "It is haunted. We're the ghosts, remember?"

"Oh, yeah, right. You know what I mean. We're still no closer to finding the Rescuer."

"Who's the Rescuer?" said a small girl, who had emerged from the shadows and quietly crept up behind them.

This time both Morph and Norman jumped clean off the ground and spun to face the child standing only a short distance away. Her matted, brunette hair rested gently on her shoulders. A light-coloured, grubby t-shirt hung loosely above a pair of ill-fitting jeans that had seen better days.

Norman estimated that she couldn't have been more than ten and had been evidently sleeping rough on the streets of Pisa for some time. Despite the ramshackle appearance, her soft brown eyes glistened brightly in the moonlight. An inquisitive look danced from Morph to Norman and back again, leaving the Ghosteleers stunned into silence.

Eventually, Morph broke the quiet. "You can see us?"

"Of course I can see you. I can see lots of different things that other kids can't." She paused as if trying to reach out for a memory long forgotten. "Come to think of it, I've never seen a talking cat before."

"Hi, I'm Norman," said Norman, extending his hand gently towards the girl.

With some hesitation, the girl reached out and clasped Norman's hand. A warm glow instantly passed through his entire body. It was as if he'd just had the most satisfying sleep in his life and awoken to find himself in a chocolate factory surrounded by soft pillows.

"My name is Sophia. It's nice to meet you."

"This is Morph, my companion."

Sophia gave a friendly smile and lightly stroked Morph's head, who then immediately started purring.

"Err Morph, we need to find the you-know-what."

"We've already found her," Morph said simply. "Who else can talk to ghosts and send waves of electricity through you with a touch?"

Norman's confused look slowly dissolved and then his eyes grew so wide, he looked very similar to the fish that had once got stuck up his nose.

Sophia giggled. "So, what am I meant to rescue?"

"The whole of humanity," said Morph.

"And who are you two?"

"We are both Ghosteleers who have come from the spirit world to save you from Apollyon's Horag soldier, who intends to kill you off so that you can't save the planet."

"What's a Ghosteleer?" Sophia frowned.

"It's a ghost whose purpose is to save important humans so that they can fulfil their destiny," explained Morph.

"Okay. . . and who is Apollyon?"

"In Greek, it means Destroyer. An evil, winged being hell bent on destroying humanity and their achievements. He hasn't been seen for hundreds of years, but his followers—the Horags—do his bidding in his absence."

Sophia stood motionless for a few seconds, pondering the information Morph had just brutally delivered. Finally, she looked at the Ghosteleers and shrugged her shoulders.

"Well, it should be an eventful evening then."

Chapter 15

The Encounter

Several minutes after Norman and Morph had transported through the Portal, Potts' laboratory door sprang fiercely open. Striding purposefully through the entrance came Ms Thorne followed closely by a serious-looking Silas.

An entourage of around forty cheering Ghosteleers trailed behind, all singing and dancing. Their exuberance had grown to near hysteria.

Potts quickly checked the TV screens to make sure they weren't showing the video from the drone Norman and Morph had taken.

"The information on the Rescuer is just coming across now. It will take a few minutes to assemble the data."

"Hurry up, Potts! We haven't got all day. The fate of the whole planet sits with the Rescuer and we can't afford to lose a second," admonished Ms Thorne.

Potts hurried around the control panel and started

flicking switches and turning dials. He could feel the icy stare of Ms Thorne upon him, as if she were rummaging into his very soul.

Several minutes passed before Potts declared the Portal was ready and pulled up the details of the Rescuer on the large screens dotted around the room. An audible gasp echoed around as the picture of a sweet, innocent child appeared.

"Are you sure you have the right person, Potts?" enquired Silas disbelievingly.

"Oh, quite positive," stammered Potts. "Her name is Sophia. I don't have a last name unfortunately. She was born in Italy just over ten years ago and she's fluent in Italian, English and Spanish. She was abandoned by her parents at the age of seven because she was different to other children and has been sleeping on the streets of Pisa ever since."

"Okay," said Silas, striding off towards the Portal. "I'm off to save the world!"

"Wait!" Ms Thorne continued to glare at Potts suspiciously. Her eyes narrowed so that only two dark slits remained. "There's something not quite right here."

Potts held his breath. He could feel sweat forming on the brow of his head as if the temperature had suddenly increased to a million degrees.

Does she know I've already sent two Ghosteleers through the Portal? Does she have special powers I don't know about?

"Ms Thorne, I'm already late," pleaded Silas. "The Horag may be attacking the child at this very moment. We have to be quick."

"Very well. But I'm coming with you," announced Ms Thorne to the surprise and delight of the collected Ghosteleers in the room, who clapped and cheered wildly.

She grabbed a Messenger device off the wall, strapped it to her wrist and instructed Potts to load it with the same settings as Silas. Potts nodded and waved the WOMBLE wand over both Silas' and Ms Thorne's Messengers, as instructed.

With the final preparations complete, Ms Thorne and Silas briskly marched towards the Portal with the sound of jubilant cheers ringing in their ears. History was about to be made.

The moment they disappeared through the shimmering haze of the Portal, Potts picked up a remote control and switched on all the TV screens in the laboratory. As the video of the horrific scene played, he was sorely tempted to turn them off again. But he didn't. Instead, he stood transfixed watching the images with the rest of the Ghosteleer community.

*

Meanwhile, Norman and Morph stood with Sophia at the base of the leaning tower, debating the best place to hide. They were too exposed out in the open, but there were too many risks if they moved to a built-up area of the city. In the end, they collectively decided to leave the appropriately named 'Square of Miracles' for somewhere a little less visible. But their time had run out.

A Horag, bigger than any they had ever seen previously,

emerged from the glooms behind the Cathedral, situated next to the tower.

The hideous creature grunted and snuffled in revulsion as it cast its black eyes towards them. Even though it stood some way off, the foul stench of its breath wafted through the stale air, making the threesome retch.

As they turned in the opposite direction, hoping they could outrun the foul beast, a darkness blacker than a crypt fell across the landscape. The temperature dropped ten degrees and a feeling of terror ripped through the night like a knife.

Standing in front of them was the gigantic figure of Apollyon. Two twisted horns were perched on top of his skeleton-like face. His burning eyes appeared to be balls of fire buried deep into their sockets. Jagged, sharp teeth protruded where lips should have been. His pale, muscular body stood over ten feet tall and appeared almost transparent. You could see the bones and organs jiggling as he arched his back, stretching his enormous frame. At the tips of his fingers, vulture-like talons grew, each ending with a razor-sharp point. Every claw was covered in poisonous green slime that slowly dripped on to the muddy floor. A pair of huge black wings appeared from his back and spread out like a ripple in an oil spill.

Norman, Morph and Sophia were rooted to the spot. Fear had paralysed them, so they were no more active than the statues that adorned the nearby Cathedral.

Suddenly, the gloom lifted slightly as a pale blue light

broke through the air. The portal door opened and out stepped the heroic figures of Silas and Ms Thorne.

Norman felt a surge of relief. They were saved! The cavalry had arrived. This was his moment to speak up for the power of goodness against the tyranny of evil that plagued parts of the world.

"Ha! Your wicked days are over Polygon," mocked Norman in front of the gargantuan horned being. "Do you know who these truly powerful people are? Silas, the best Ghosteleer in modern times and this—," Norman extended his arm. "This is the legendary Ms Thorne, President of the Ghosteleers and holder of every record there is. Between them, they've saved more humans than you can possibly imagine."

"Err, Norman?" enquired Morph.

"Not now Morph. I'm on a roll. This is my moment of glory," whispered Norman.

"It's four against two, Polygon. Turn around and crawl back down to the pit you belong in and take your smelly Horag with you." Norman raised his chin in a triumphant gesture and waited for Apollyon to turn-tail and leave.

Instead, the creature swivelled his bony head and looked Ms Thorne square in the eyes.

"You're late. You and Silas should have been here ages ago. And who is this idiot who can't even pronounce my name?"

Norman's mouth fell open in shock. *How could he already know Ms Thorne and Silas?* Very slowly, the penny dropped.

Ms Thorne rolled her eyes and addressed Apollyon. "That moron Potts delayed us and now I know why." She threw Morph and Norman an angry, piercing look. "He'll be having an appointment with my dagger when I return."

Still with her attention fixed firmly on Norman and Morph, her face lightened slightly.

"It was very good of you to find the Rescuer for us. Saves a lot of time. I'll make your deaths quick, as soon as I dispose of the girl."

*

Back in the lab, the questioning glances the Ghosteleers had hurled at Potts, evaporated. At first, there were huge cheers for Norman's rousing speech. Sir Poop, who had arrived earlier with Tabris, Nick and Lynn, even shed a tear of pride. But the revelation that Ms Thorne and Silas were both in cahoots with the mighty Apollyon brought a deathly silence, previously unknown in the facility. They had been betrayed by the most trusted of individuals.

"Potts! Get me in there, quick!" screamed Tabris.

"It's not possible! There's a limit to the number of Ghosteleers that can be sent through the portal to the same place at the same time. If anyone else goes through it will cause a molecular meltdown!"

Tabris stood in shock, frustration ripping through every fibre of her body. There was nothing they could do other than watch it play out on the giant TV screens.

Chapter 16

The Battle

"But why go against every Ghosteleer principle? Why join with the forces of evil?" Morph questioned.

"It's quite simple really," stated Ms Thorne, who remained completely oblivious that their conversation was being transmitted live to the Ghosteleer facility. "It comes down to money and power. You see our budgets keep getting cut every year, because Ghosteleers are becoming more efficient, faster and smarter. So, we don't need as many, which isn't great for building my empire. That's why I recruited Norman here. To bring down the average intelligence, allowing me to make an argument that I still need the money to train morons like him."

Norman felt like a blade of ice had pierced his heart. He stood open-mouthed and mortified that he had been used so blatantly by Ms Thorne. She merely smiled at him like he was a naughty puppy.

"Oh, don't take it too badly Norman. You were my ideal Ghosteleer. A useless fool, barely able to tie your own shoelaces. You couldn't fight off a cold, let alone a Horag."

Norman's shoulders slumped. He couldn't have felt any more crestfallen.

"But then the Rescuer turns up earlier than I expected. How many Ghosteleers do you think we'll need if she survives? She can even see us! God only knows what other power she possesses. And when she eventually dies, where do you think she will go?"

"She'll take my rightful position as your successor and *future* President of the Ghosteleers," spat Silas in disdain.

"That's right," agreed Ms Thorne. "She'll destroy the Ghosteleers and put what in its place? Peace and harmony? Ha! Humans don't want peace; they enjoy fighting too much."

"But our motto," persisted Norman. " 'One for all and all for one.' Doesn't that mean anything to you?"

"Oh, you idiot! That's the Musketeers. The Ghosteleer's motto is, 'all for me.' " Ms Thorne chuckled lightly at her attempt of a joke.

"Enough talking!" roared the deep, gravelly voice of Apollyon. "The girl's a threat to all of us. The quicker she dies the better."

"Stand aside Norman and Morph! Let us do our business," Silas said.

Morph dug his claws into the ground, arched his back and hissed louder than Norman had ever heard.

"We're not going to let you," retorted Norman, whose feeling of deflation had transformed to anger.

"It makes no difference," said Ms Thorne casually.

She looked at Silas and then up at the tower, still glistening in the moonlight. He nodded his understanding and a wicked smile grew on his face.

The pair lifted their arms and started walking backwards, away from the soaring column of stone. Instantly, a low rumble shook the ground. It became louder and more powerful, as if someone were turning the dial up on a machine that creates earthquakes.

A huge slab of marble crashed into the earth just in front of Sophia, propelling dirt high into the air. Morph spun around. Apollyon and the Horag were blocking their exit. Silas and Ms Thorne were trying to bury Sophia under the toppled Leaning Tower of Pisa.

"Norman! Get Sophia and crouch down behind me!" Morph shouted.

Rapidly, stones started raining from the sky. At first, a few pillars fell, then larger pieces, followed by a thunderous roar of huge, heavy blocks booming into the ground. The ear-splitting sound shook the whole square, like a war between Gods, until every block had fallen.

Eventually, silence returned. Beneath the vast cloud of dust that had swallowed the Field of Miracles, lay the buried bodies of Norman, Morph and Sophia.

*

"No!" cried Potts and Tabris in unison.

The remainder of the Ghosteleers stood quietly, staring in

disbelief at the screens dotted around the lab. The legendary Rescuer had died. For centuries, the fabled story foretold this special person healing the rifts in the world. And now she was gone. Killed by the hands of the highest-ranking Ghosteleers sworn to protect her.

*

Silas smiled contentedly at the mass of stone heaped on top of the Rescuer. The dust had finally started to disperse and drift with the wind. The collapse of the iconic tower had settled the fate of the Rescuer, but Silas wanted to finish off Morph as well. He knew the pathetic moggy would come crawling out through the rocks at any moment.

Silas reached inside his coat pocket and carefully withdrew the golden dagger used during the Passing Away ceremony. Even in the moonlight, the jewels sparkled ominously. One stab and the cat would be gone forever.

"Here kitty, kitty, kitty. Look what I have for you!" taunted Silas.

Coughing and spluttering under the heaps of stones, Morph looked around. Norman was kneeling, sheltering Sophia in a cocoon made of marble and lime. Morph had managed to arrange all the falling stones into an igloo shaped dome that protected them from the barrage of tumbling debris.

Sophia, completely unhurt, peeked through her arms, which were tightly wrapped over her head. Norman did the same, although being a ghost, he didn't really need to.

"I have an idea," Morph explained hurriedly. "But I need

both of you to help me. Norman, remember our power is stronger when we're together?" Norman nodded. "Well, we're going to surprise the living daylights out of those evil fiends and show them we're a force to be reckoned with. Norman, hold Sophia's hand. Sophia, grab my tail."

Once the connection had been made, a surge of energy skipped through Morph's feline body. The transformation was like shifting from a candle to a nuclear reactor that had just been turned to maximum. He felt invincible. His whiskers twitched, his claws extended, and he closed his eyes, focusing all his strength on the enormous pile of stones above. Very slowly, the slabs of marble, most weighing more than a car, started to float steadily upwards.

Apollyon was standing next to Ms Thorne and Silas when the first block began stirring. All three stared in disbelief as stone after stone started rising softly into the night air. After several minutes, hundreds of huge boulders circled overhead, elegantly dancing among the bright stars.

Morph swished his paw back and forth like a conductor orchestrating a thousand-piece rock band. One by one, each piece of rubble gently rotated and slotted back in its original place. The magical tower of Pisa started to grow like a beanstalk, stretching high into the sky. Eventually, with a final flick of his paw, the Italian flag capped the tall building and began waving lightly in the breeze.

Ms Thorne started a slow and deliberate clap. "I'm impressed Morph. I had no idea you had such skill. But I bet you're feeling pretty tired now. It's such a shame we have to put you down."

Sophia dropped Morph's tail and took two paces back from the advancing Silas, who still gripped the golden dagger in his outstretched hand. Morph instantly collapsed to the floor in exhaustion, unable to even move a whisker.

"Morph!" shouted Norman in alarm.

"Run!" whispered the weak response from Morph, just before he passed out.

*

The mood in the lab had lifted considerably when the first stones started moving. Ghosteleers pointed at the screens in wonderment; thrilled that the trio had not only survived but were showing incredible resilience. But the balance had tilted again.

Silas, once their hero, was advancing menacingly with the dagger aimed at Morph who remained motionless on the dusty ground.

Potts shook with anger as Silas crept ever closer to his best friend's limp body. In a few seconds, Morph would be gone forever.

He spun quickly and slammed the palm of his hand on a large red button located at the bottom of the control panel.

*

As Silas drew back the dagger, ready to plunge it towards his bothersome enemy, his Messenger device started beeping, as did the one attached to Ms Thorne.

"Oh, that Potts is insufferable!" exclaimed Ms Thorne. "He's got the timing all wrong. I'll go back, reset the clock for sixty minutes and then return, so we can settle this mess once and for all."

With that, she pressed the Portal reactivation button on her Messenger. But nothing happened. She pressed it harder, stabbing at the button stubbornly until her nail chipped. Still the Portal door did not appear.

"Silas, you try. Mine appears to be broken."

Silas pressed the button on his Messenger, only to receive the same non-responsive result. The beeping noise became louder and faster. He reached out to Morph's Messenger, but again, nothing happened. Silas looked up at Ms Thorne in alarm.

"Quick, grab Norman's Messenger! We'll use his."

Pouncing like a leopard, Silas raced towards Norman at frightening speed. Norman snatched Sophia's hand, turned and ran as fast as he could towards the Cathedral. He could hear the beeping noise behind him getting increasingly louder as Silas closed the gap.

Sophia tripped just as they approached the main entrance and sprawled painfully on the floor, clutching her ankle. Norman shuddered to a halt and turned to face the rushing Silas, whose Messenger device had started making an alarming high-pitched sound.

Silas sprang like a possessed madman aiming for Norman's wrist. Norman could feel a rush of air as

Silas reached out desperately to grab the button that would activate the Portal and save his life. But Silas was a fingertip too short. He dissolved instantly, staring hatefully into Norman's eyes.

A short distance away, Ms Thorne stood petrified, looking pleadingly at Apollyon for assistance. He simply shrugged his large broad shoulders and stared at her with his empty, fiery eyes.

"Blast you, Potts!" screamed Ms Thorne before she melted into nothing.

Apollyon growled in frustration and turned to the Horag, who remained silent by his side.

"I want you to tear that embarrassment of a Ghosteleer to shreds and then kill the girl."

Norman could see, and smell, the approaching Horag, rapidly bounding towards him across the grass. Its teeth were bared and snarling like a rabid dog in search of a steak dinner. A glint of pure malevolence filled its black eyes. Faster and faster it descended upon Norman.

Norman stood bravely in front of the crouching Sophia, who remained on the ground, rubbing her sore ankle. Norman knew his time was up, but he wasn't going to leave Sophia to this wicked creature.

He steadied himself for the impact of the Horag, which leaped at him with all its force. Norman shut his eyes, waiting for the blow to knock him off his feet, but nothing happened.

Slowly, he opened an eyelid, turned and saw an equally puzzled Horag dissolve in front of him. Stuck to the bottom of its foot was the golden dagger Silas had dropped onto the grass after lunging at Norman.

"Do you know what? I really think this place is the Square of Miracles." Sophia smiled and stood tentatively on her ankle.

Apollyon let out a thunderous roar that shook every building in sight, threatening to collapse the tower once again. He spread his huge wings, stretched out his powerful arms and stamped angrily across the ground towards Norman, who quickly picked up the dagger.

"Sophia, run!" Norman urged.

Sophia hesitated for a split second, then turned and hobbled towards the back of the Cathedral, disappearing from sight.

Norman backed gradually away until he felt the cold, solid wall of the Cathedral press firmly against his back. Without Morph, he certainly couldn't use his powers. Even if he did have them, they were no match against Apollyon, who stopped a short distance in front of him, blocking off any possible escape.

Up close, Norman could clearly see the creature's expanding lungs, beating black heart and muscles flexing through his transparent skin. Norman summoned every grain of courage for his final stand.

"You've lost Polygon. The Ghosteleer betrayers are gone and I've defeated your Horag. Leave the girl alone."

Apollyon sneered. "I've lost nothing you fool. She will still die tonight and the human race will fall."

Norman quickly dove the dagger deep into Apollyon's

leg. It was like plunging a spoon into jelly and seemed to have the same effect. Apollyon lifted his head and laughed so loudly that the ground trembled. As he did so, the inside of his body jiggled wildly.

"You can't hurt me with that toy. Don't you know who I am? Do you not know the power I have? I am the Destroyer!" His deep, husky voice boomed around the square.

He lifted one of his gigantic hands and scratched his talons across the wall of the Cathedral, sending sparks flying and cutting deep scores into the marble. Green slime oozed out of his claws, which hissed like acid, as it touched the stone.

Norman covered his ears; the sound turned his blood cold.

"There've been hundreds of brave Ghosteleers who have screamed for mercy when just one of my claws has scratched their skin. Imagine the pain that a weakling like you will feel."

"You don't scare me," Norman said defiantly. "I may not be the strongest, smartest, fastest, most skilful Ghosteleer that ever walked, but I've always stood up to bullies and I'll stand up to you."

Apollyon stretched out his dripping claws and raised his hands above his head, ready to strike down upon Norman, who stood with his back against the wall, silhouetted in the moonlight.

Just as the poisonous talons started falling, Sophia rushed at Apollyon from behind and plunged her hand deep into his back. Norman could see her tiny fingers pushing through the jelly, gripping Apollyon's black, beating heart, which immediately started to glow a warm red.

Apollyon let out a tremendous howl as the goodness that coursed through Sophia's body trickled into the evil monster. The more he wailed, the tighter her grip became and the brighter his heart shone.

Apollyon twisted agonisingly, desperate to escape the torture, but Sophia hung on determinedly. His great black wings fluttered like a crow caught in a net and his flaming eyes grew to large balls of fire. With a final, curdling cry, Apollyon exploded into a million points of light that spread rapidly outwards, knocking both Sophia and Norman off their feet.

For a moment, they both sat staring at each other, wondering whether they would suddenly wake up from a fitful sleep. Then Norman remembered his dear friend lying unconscious on the dusty ground near the tower.

"Morph! I'm coming!"

The pair raced over to Morph. Sophia laid her hand gently on his side and after several seconds, Morph slowly opened his eyes. He peered up at the couple looking eagerly upon him.

"Have I died again?"

"No Morph, you're alive. Well, you're still dead, but only the once."

Norman picked Morph up in his arms and cradled him like a baby. He then looked gratefully at Sophia who produced a large smile that warmed the hearts of the Ghosteleers.

Norman pressed the button on his Messenger device and instantly the blue shimmering window appeared. He looked up with a final glance at the tower.

"Err, Morph. The Leaning Tower of Pisa is now straight."

"I know," croaked Morph weakly. "I thought this way it would look like a giant scratching post like the one I had when I was a kitten."

"Oh, okay, fair enough. I guess they'll get used to it."

They gave Sophia a big hug.

"Thank you for everything," Sophia said.

The familiar, high-pitched sound of the drone descended and the Ghosteleers returned through the Portal, exhausted but victorious.

Chapter 17

The Reception

As Norman stepped through the Portal, gently carrying Morph in his arms, an enormous cheer erupted. Word had spread quickly through the facility about the unfolding events being shown on the TV monitors and every Ghosteleer had crammed into the lab to witness the incredible scenes for themselves.

Norman, clearly startled, looked around in fright, feeling that he had mistakenly stood in front of an honoured guest. However, as he wrestled his way towards Potts, standing by the control panel, his fear turned to relief. Complete strangers pushed their way forward wanting to congratulate him and Morph, who still lay semi-conscious in his arms.

Norman laid Morph gently on a wooden counter and the crowd began to edge back a little. Potts opened a first aid kit labelled 'Morph' and retrieved a small green bottle, which he carefully unscrewed and wafted under Morph's nose.

A millisecond later, his whiskers twitched excitedly and his tail shot straight out like a spring-loaded pogo-stick. Quickly, Potts screwed the lid back on the bottle, hid it away in an air-tight casing and locked it in a nearby safe.

Morph opened his eyes, jumped to his feet and started prowling the table hungrily, sniffing every centimetre of the surface.

"Catnip infused with chicken," Potts whispered quietly to Norman. "Thought it might help him get back on his feet. Don't worry, the effects will wear off soon."

"Make way please!" Sir Poop shouted through the lively crowd, who dutifully started parting like the Red Sea. Tabris followed closely behind.

As he reached Norman, he extended his arms wide to embrace him in a big celebratory hug, but then stopped at the last moment and withdrew a leather bag from his jacket. Sir Poop then reached very carefully into Norman's pocket and pulled out the golden dagger by its handle.

"Don't want to have an accident now, do we?"

Once the dagger had been safely tucked away, he threw his arms around Norman. He then turned to Morph, who had calmed a little by this point, and proceed to give him an energetic stroke of the head.

"I've notified the High Council of the developments here tonight and representatives will be arriving at any minute." Sir Poop still looked visibly shaken by the evening's revelations and began to wipe his brow with a not-so-clean handkerchief that he whipped from his sleeve.

Morph had almost recovered his strength, which gave Norman the opportunity to fill him in on the recent proceedings.

"So, technically, Potts removed Silas and Ms Thorne, the Horag accidentally defeated itself by standing on the dagger and Sophia overcame Apollyon single-handed. Does that sound about right?" Morph summarised.

"No!" cried Tabris. "Norman was magnificent! Unbelievably brave! He took on the Horag and Apollyon without flinching once and protected Sophia throughout. He's a hero!"

Norman felt his face rapidly resemble a bright, red, chilli pepper. Behind him, a horde of Ghosteleers applauded passionately, obviously agreeing with Tabris' sentiment.

"Tabris, do you think we could try that kiss again please?" Norman quietly questioned and Tabris nodded shyly.

They kissed to the surprise and delight of everyone, and this time, they didn't bang heads painfully.

*

Two days later, a lavish award ceremony was arranged in the large conference room. The High Council, comprising five unlikely individuals, were seated behind a large table in the centre of the stage.

Mrs Peacock was situated on the far left. Strangely, she had a real peacock sitting on her head that wobbled when she agreed with the comments of her colleagues.

Next to her, sitting very upright indeed, was Mr

Boggsworth, an ex-headmaster with beady eyes hidden behind large, round-rimmed glasses.

Further along sat Miss Symonds, a grizzled and leather-faced adventurer who'd swum the Amazon twice in her lifetime, just to pass the time.

Last but one, was the bubbly Mrs Yat, who simply couldn't stop talking, even if it was to herself and finally, at the far right of the table, sat a tall, serious-looking man dressed in an old Abraham Lincoln costume.

Norman felt extremely nervous being one of the guests of honour at the award ceremony and tried to joke with the man about his ridiculous, old-fashioned clothing. Unfortunately for Norman, it turned out he was the real Abraham Lincoln and didn't have much of a sense of humour.

Mr Boggsworth stood, thrusting his chest out. He cleared his throat and the room fell silent. Gripped in his hands was a set of barely legible scribbles.

"Today, we honour the exceptionally gifted Morph and the remarkably brave Norman."

A generous ripple of applause drifted through the room.

"Our true colours shine brightest in the darkest shadows and Norman has survived those shadows. That is why I can't help but think of him as a cow pat."

Norman's mouth dropped open. Mr Boggsworth paused, adjusted his glasses, held his notes a little closer and quickly corrected himself. "I'm sorry, I meant that I think of him as an owl or bat. Both courageous creatures that survive at night."

Norman reclosed his mouth.

"Thanks to the heroics of this pair, the future of the human race and the Ghosteleers is very bright indeed."

Mr Boggsworth made no mention of the treacherous traitors that had tainted the Ghosteleer reputation.

After many more flattering comments, Norman and Morph were invited to the front and presented with golden medals of valour. The jubilant audience clapped enthusiastically, especially Tabris, Sir Poop, Nick and Lynn who instigated a standing ovation.

The awards came to an end shortly afterwards and the guests dispersed back into the main facility.

"Norman and Morph?" enquired Mr Boggsworth. "Would you mind waiting a second please?"

He paused until the room had completely emptied and then spoke in a secretive, hushed voice. "I have recently received information of a very delicate nature."

Mr Boggsworth hesitated and looked around, making absolutely sure they were completely alone. "I would like you two to travel into the after-after life and retrieve the Lakeshia map from the Architect. It's going to be extremely dangerous. There are many more wicked creatures out there other than Apollyon. With your skills and bravery, I believe you can achieve it."

Norman's smile stretched so wide his cheeks hurt. He had never felt so proud. A new adventure was about to begin. . .

The End

Ghosteleer Gazette Exclusive

Gerri Golightly grills Norman

Gerri: You've defeated one of the toughest villains in the universe, saved the Rescuer of humanity and revived your unconscious cat. How did you possibly manage it?

Norman: Oh, it's quite simple really. I have no idea. My eyes were shut for most of it.

Gerri: When did you first realise that Ms Thorne and Silas were working with Apollyon?

Norman: I became suspicious when Ms Thorne started talking to Polygon and calling me an idiot. Afterwards, when she dropped the Leaning Tower of Pizza on my head, I really thought something wasn't right.

Gerri: At one point you were only seconds away from a very painful death. What was going through your mind?

Norman: How that sock got behind my oven before I blew myself up. I'm not even sure it was mine.

Gerri: Some people believe you will become one of the very best Ghosteleers we've ever had. Where do you see yourself in a year's time?

Norman: On holiday, hopefully somewhere far away.

Gerri: So, what do you have planned for the future?

Norman: If I wasn't dead, lunch.

Gerri: No, I mean long term?

Norman: Oh, in that case dinner, followed by dessert.

About the Author

Philip Beicken was born in Galway, Ireland but moved to England when he was six months old. He lives in West Sussex with his wife and two children and spends most of his time clearing up the mess made by the growing number of animals his daughter adopts. Included in that list are two kittens named Molly and Marley, who like nothing more than chasing every leaf, butterfly and frog in the garden.

Even at an early age, Philip enjoyed creating fast paced, light-hearted stories filled with heroes, heroines and villains. His love of sports, especially tennis and badminton, keeps him active for large spells during the week. When he's not writing, he runs his own business as a 360 videographer, which has enabled him to film in the USA and Europe.

Find out more at www.philipbeicken.com
Follow Philip on Twitter: @PBeicken
Instagram: @pbeickenauthor

The
Ghosteleers